P9-DMJ-462

Adam followed Clare down the steps.

Her head was bent as she navigated the narrow stairs, exposing the delicate nape of her neck. It made her seem vulnerable. And fragile. And awakened a protective instinct in him. He'd experienced a similar feeling about his late wife. But it had been long absent from his life. Nor did it make any sense now.

For so many years, the only woman in his life had been his daughter, Nicole. Worrying about her had consumed his thoughts and energies. He'd rarely given any other female more than a passing glance.

Now Clare would be living in his backyard. As she'd noted, it was a business arrangement, nothing more. And he would do well to remember that. Even if he was inclined to consider her in a more personal light, it would be a mistake. It was a mistake he'd made once before, and he didn't intend to repeat it. It wouldn't be fair to any woman.

Because he just wasn't husband material....

Books by Irene Hannon

Love Inspired

Home for the Holidays #6
A Groom of Her Own #16
A Family To Call Her Own #25
It Had To Be You #58
One Special Christmas #77
The Way Home #112
Never Say Goodbye #175
Crossroads #224
†*The Best Gift* #292
†*Gift from the Heart* #307

*Vows
†Sisters & Brides

IRENE HANNON

is an award-winning author who has been a writer for as long as she can remember. She "officially" launched her career at the age of ten, when she was one of the winners in a "complete-the-story" contest conducted by a national children's magazine. More recently, Irene won the coveted RITA® Award for her 2002 Love Inspired book *Never Say Goodbye*. Irene, who spent many years in an executive corporate communications position with a Fortune 500 company, now devotes herself full-time to her writing career. In her "spare" time, she enjoys performing in community musical theater productions, singing in the church choir, gardening, cooking and spending time with family and friends. She and her husband, Tom—whom she describes as "my own romantic hero"—make their home in Missouri.

GIFT FROM THE HEART

IRENE HANNON

Steeple
Hill®

Published by Steeple Hill Books™

If you purchased this book without a cover you should be aware that this book is stolen property. It was reported as "unsold and destroyed" to the publisher, and neither the author nor the publisher has received any payment for this "stripped book."

STEEPLE HILL BOOKS

Steeple Hill®

ISBN 0-373-87317-4

GIFT FROM THE HEART

Copyright © 2005 by Irene Hannon

All rights reserved. Except for use in any review, the reproduction or utilization of this work in whole or in part in any form by any electronic, mechanical or other means, now known or hereafter invented, including xerography, photocopying and recording, or in any information storage or retrieval system, is forbidden without the written permission of the editorial office, Steeple Hill Books, 233 Broadway, New York, NY 10279 U.S.A.

All characters in this book have no existence outside the imagination of the author and have no relation whatsoever to anyone bearing the same name or names. They are not even distantly inspired by any individual known or unknown to the author, and all incidents are pure invention.

This edition published by arrangement with Steeple Hill Books.

® and TM are trademarks of Steeple Hill Books, used under license. Trademarks indicated with ® are registered in the United States Patent and Trademark Office, the Canadian Trade Marks Office and in other countries.

www.SteepleHill.com

Printed in U.S.A.

For You have tested us, O God! You have tried us as silver is tried by fire; You have brought us into a snare; You laid a heavy burden on our back. You let men ride over our heads; we went through fire and water, but You have led us out to refreshment.

—*Psalms* 66:10–12

To my wonderful husband, Tom, who supported my decision to leave the corporate world and follow my dream. Thank you—always—for your gifts of love and encouragement.

Prologue

Clare Randall drew a shaky breath and reached up with trembling fingers to tuck a stray strand of honey-gold hair back into her elegant chignon. With a sigh, she transferred her gaze from the brilliant St. Louis late-October sky outside the window to the interior of the legal offices of Mitchell and Montgomery. Normally, the hushed, elegant setting would have calmed her. As it was, the tranquil ambiance created by the dove-gray carpeting, rich mahogany wainscoting and subdued lighting did little to settle her turbulent emotions.

Still, she couldn't help noticing that Seth Mitchell, Aunt Jo's attorney, had good taste. Or at least his decorator did. The Lladro figurine displayed on a lighted shelf was exquisite, the Waterford bowl beside it stunning. Yet the beautiful items left her feeling only sad and melancholy, for they reminded her of another time, another life, when her world had been filled with such expensive objects. A life that now seemed only a distant memory as she struggled just to eke out a living.

Suddenly the door to the inner office opened, and three heads swiveled in unison toward the attorney.

Please, Lord, let this be the answer to my prayers! Clare pleaded in fervent silence as her fingers tightened convulsively on the tissue in her lap.

But the distinguished, gray-haired man who paused on the threshold didn't appear to be in any hurry to disclose the contents of Jo Warren's last will and testament as he gave each of her great-nieces a slow, discerning appraisal.

Clare wondered how they fared as she, too, turned to contemplate her sisters. A.J., the youngest, was tall and lean, with long, naturally curly strawberry-blond hair too unruly to be tamed even by strategically placed combs. Her calf-length skirt and long tunic top, cinched at the waist with an unusual metal belt, were somewhat eclectic, but the attire suited her free-spirited personality. She seemed curious and interested as she gazed back at Seth Mitchell.

Clare looked toward Morgan. Her middle sister wore her dark copper-colored hair in a sleek, shoulder-length style, and her chic business attire screamed big city and success. She was looking at the attorney with a bored, impatient, let's-get-on-with-this-because-I-have-better-things-to-do look.

And how did Seth Mitchell view her? Clare wondered, as she turned back to him. Did he see the deep, lingering sadness in the depths of her eyes? Or did he only notice her designer suit and Gucci purse—remnants of a life that had vanished one fateful day two years ago.

She had no time to ponder those questions, because suddenly her great-aunt's attorney moved toward them. "Good morning, ladies. I'm Seth Mitchell. I recognize you from Jo's description—A.J., Morgan, Clare," he said, correctly identifying the sisters as he extended his hand to each in turn. "Please accept my condolences on the loss of your aunt. She was a great lady."

They murmured polite responses, and he motioned toward his office. "If you're ready, we can proceed with the reading of the will."

Clare paused to reach for her purse, glancing at her sisters as they passed by. Morgan was looking at her watch, clearly anxious to get to the airport in plenty of time for her flight back to Boston and the high-stakes advertising world she inhabited. A.J. had slowed her step to take another look at the flame-red maples outside the window.

Clare shook her head and an affectionate smile tugged at the corners of her mouth. No two sisters could be more different. A.J. always took time to smell the flowers; Morgan didn't even notice them. And their personalities had clashed in other ways, too. As the oldest, Clare had spent much of her youth acting as mediator between the two of them. Yet the three sisters shared an enduring bond, one that had only been strengthened as they'd clung together through A.J.'s tragedy.

And her own.

As Clare followed her sisters into the attorney's office, her spirits nosedived. The past two years had tested her faith—and her finances—to the breaking point. Her work as a substitute teacher barely kept her solvent, and loneliness—especially during the endless, dark nights when sleep was elusive—was her constant companion. With A.J. living in Chicago, Morgan in Boston and Clare in Kansas City, their contact was largely confined to periodic telephone chats. Which was better than nothing. But not enough. For the past couple of days, as they'd come together to mourn and pay tribute to their great-aunt,

Clare had felt a sense of comfort, of love, of warmth that had long been absent from her life. She would miss them when they all returned to their own lives.

Tears pricked her eyelids again, and she blinked them back fiercely, fighting to maintain control. Crying didn't help anything. It was just a selfish exercise in self-indulgence. Especially when she had no one to blame for her situation except herself. Focus on the present, she told herself resolutely as she took a steadying breath. Just concentrate on what Aunt Jo's attorney has to say and put regrets aside for a few minutes.

Seth Mitchell waited until the three women were seated, then picked up a hefty document. "I'll give each of you a copy of your great-aunt's will to take with you, so I don't think there's any reason to go through this whole document now. A lot of it is legalese, and there are some charitable bequests that you can review at your leisure. I thought we could restrict the formal reading to the section that affects each of you directly, if that's agreeable."

Morgan quickly replied in the affirmative, making it clear that she was in a hurry. Then, as if realizing she may have overstepped, she sent her older sister a questioning look. Clare nodded her assent, struck as always by Morgan's focus on her job. Clare had enjoyed her teaching career, but she hadn't built her life around it. Nor had A.J. put success—in a worldly sense—at the top of her priority list. Clare wasn't sure why Morgan had become so focused on making the big bucks. But maybe she should take a lesson from her middle sister, she acknowledged with a sigh. Because she could use some big bucks about now. Or even some small bucks, for that matter. That's why Aunt Jo's bequest seemed the answer to a prayer.

As Seth flipped through the document to a marked page and began to read, Clare forced herself to pay attention.

"Insofar as I have no living relatives other than my three great-nieces—the daughters of my sole nephew, Jonathan Williams, now deceased—I bequeath the bulk of my estate to them in the following manner and with the following stipulations and conditions.

"To Abigail Jeanette Williams, I bequeath half ownership of my bookstore in St. Louis, Turning Leaves, with the stipulation that she retain ownership for a minimum of six months and work full-time in the store during this period. The remaining half ownership I bequeath to the present manager, Blake Sullivan, with the same stipulation.

"To Morgan Williams, I bequeath half ownership of Serenity Point, my cottage in Seaside, Maine, providing that she retains her ownership for a six-month period following my death and that she spends a total of four weeks in residence at the cottage. During this time she is also to provide advertising and promotional assistance for Good Shepherd Camp and attend board meetings as an advisory member. The remaining half ownership of the cottage I bequeath to Grant Kincaid of Seaside, Maine.

"To Clare Randall, I bequeath my remaining financial assets, except for those designated to be given to the charities specified in this document, with the stipulation that she serve as nanny for Nicole Wright, daughter of Dr. Adam Wright of Hope Creek, North Carolina, for a period of six months, at no charge to Dr. Wright.

"Should the stipulations and conditions for the aforementioned bequests not be fulfilled, the specified assets will be disposed of according to directions given to my attorney, Seth Mitchell. He will also designate the date on which the clock will begin ticking on the six-month period specified in my will."

Seth lowered the document to his desk and looked at the women across from him.

"There you have it, ladies. I can provide more details on your bequests to each of you individually, but are there any general questions that I can answer?"

Clare vaguely heard the disgust in Morgan's voice as she made some comment about the impossibility of getting away from the office for four days, let alone four weeks. A.J., on her other hand, sounded excited about the bookshop and eager to tackle a new challenge. But Clare was too caught up in her own bequest to pay much attention to her sisters' questions.

"Who is this Dr. Wright?" Clare asked with a frown. "And what makes Aunt Jo think he would want me as a nanny?"

"Dr. Wright is an old friend of Jo's from St. Louis. I believe she met him through her church, and even when he moved to North Carolina, they remained close friends," Seth told Clare. "He's a widower with an eleven-year-old daughter who apparently needs guidance and closer supervision. As to why Jo thought Dr. Wright would be interested in having you as a nanny, I can't say."

He paused and glanced at his desk calendar. "Let's officially start the clock for the six-month period on December first. That will give you about a month to make plans. Now, are there any more general questions?"

When no one responded, he nodded. "Very well." He handed them each a manila envelope. "But do feel free to call if any come up as you review the will more thoroughly." He rose and extended his hand to each sister in turn. "Again, my condolences on the death of your great-aunt. Jo had a positive impact on countless lives and will be missed by many people. I know she loved each of you very much, and that she wanted you to succeed in claiming your bequests. Good luck, ladies."

The three sisters exited Seth Mitchell's office silently, each lost in her own thoughts. When Clare had been notified that she'd been named as a beneficiary in Aunt Jo's will, she'd just assumed that her great aunt had left her a small amount of cash—enough, she hoped, to tide her over until she got her teaching career reestablished. She certainly hadn't expected a six-figure bequest. Or one that came with strings.

None of them had.

She glanced at her sisters. A.J. looked enthusiastic and energized. But then, she was always up for some new adventure, and she had no real ties to Chicago. It would be easy for her to move and start a new life. Morgan, on the other hand, looked put out. To claim her inheritance, she'd have to find a way to juggle the demands of her career with the stipulations in the will. And that wouldn't be easy.

As for Clare—she was just confused. She'd never been to North Carolina, had no experience as a nanny and had never heard of this Dr. Wright. It wasn't that she minded moving; she had nothing to hold her in Kansas City now. Yet wouldn't this man think it odd if she just showed up on his doorstep and offered to be his daughter's nanny?

But Clare needed Aunt Jo's inheritance. She had to find a way to make this work.

As the sisters paused outside Seth Mitchell's office, each preparing to go her own way, Clare's eyes teared up once more. It might be a long time before they were together again. And different as they were, they'd always been like the Three Musketeers—one for all, and all for one.

A.J. also looked misty-eyed as she reached over to give each of her sisters a hug. "Keep in touch, okay?"

"Have fun with the bookshop," Clare told her. Then she turned to Morgan. "I hope you can work things out with the cottage."

Morgan returned her hug. "I'm not holding my breath," she said dryly.

"I'll pray for all of us," A.J. promised.

That was a good thing, Clare thought, as they parted. Because they would need all the prayers they could get.

Along with a whole lot of luck.

Chapter One

Hope Creek, North Carolina

Dr. Adam Wright wearily reached for the stack of messages on his desk and glanced at the clock, then to the early November darkness outside his window. He was already late picking up Nicole, and he knew he'd hear about it. Neither his wife nor his daughter had ever had much patience with the demands of his family practice. And things had gone from bad to worse with Nicole since she'd come to live with him a year ago. Toss awakening hormones into the mix, and it was a recipe for disaster. Which just about described his relationship with his eleven-year-old daughter, he thought with a sigh.

Adam rapidly scanned the messages. Janice had taken care of all but the most urgent in her usual efficient manner, he noted gratefully. Those that remained were from patients who really did need to speak with him. Except for the last one.

Adam frowned at the unfamiliar name and the out-of-state area code. The message was from a woman named

Clare Randall and contained just one word—*Personal*. His frown deepened. Janice usually intercepted sales-people, so he assumed this Clare Randall had convinced Janice that she had a legitimate reason for wanting to speak with him. But the message wasn't marked urgent, so it could wait until tomorrow, he decided. The other calls he'd return from home, after he picked up Nicole.

It would help pass the long evening ahead, in which he assumed his daughter would once again give him the silent treatment for his latest transgression of tardiness.

Nicole was out the door of Mrs. Scott's house even be-fore Adam's car came to a stop. The older woman ap-peared a moment later, and even from a distance Adam could see her frown. Not a good sign. He summoned up a smile and waved to his temporary babysitter, then steeled himself for the coming encounter with his daugh-ter. His stomach clenched, and he forced himself to take a deep breath as she climbed into the car and slammed the door.

"Did you thank Mrs. Scott?" he asked.

Nicole didn't look at him, and when she spoke her voice was surly—and accusatory. "Why should I? You pay her to watch me. And you're late. Again."

A muscle clenched in his jaw even as he told him-self to cut his daughter some slack. She'd lost her mother just over a year ago, been forced to live with a father she'd never quite connected with, then been up-rooted from her home and friends in St. Louis and plopped down in this small North Carolina town. At the time, Adam had thought the move back to his home state was for the best. He didn't like the crowd of friends Nicole hung out with, nor the fact that she often seemed to be eleven going on thirty. Day by day he'd felt his authority slipping away as his daughter spun out of control. So when he'd heard of the need for a doctor in Hope Creek, it had seemed like the answer to his prayers. He'd hoped that the wholesome atmosphere of small-town living would straighten Nicole out and help them bond.

Unfortunately, things hadn't worked out that way. If anything, Nicole resented him more than ever, and the gulf between them had widened. She had also become a master at evading questions and putting him on the defensive, he realized. But the ploy wasn't going to work tonight.

"The issue isn't whether or not I pay Mrs. Scott. The issue is politeness," he said firmly.

She ignored his comment. "So why were you late?"

He wasn't going to be sidetracked. He'd already been through half a dozen sitters. He was grateful that Mrs. Scott from church had taken pity on him and offered to watch Nicole until he found someone on a more permanent basis. But he hadn't had any luck on that score yet. So he couldn't afford to alienate his Good Samaritan.

"Did you thank Mrs. Scott?" he repeated more firmly.

Her jaw settled into a stubborn line, and she glared at him defiantly. "Yes."

He knew she was lying. And she knew he knew it. She was calling his bluff. And he couldn't back down. "That's good. I think I'll just go have a word with Mrs. Scott myself," he said evenly as he reached for the door handle. He was halfway out of the car before she spoke.

"Okay, so I didn't thank her," Nicole said sullenly.

Adam paused, then settled back in the car. "There's still time. She hasn't gone in yet."

Nicole gave him a venomous look, then rolled down her window. "Thanks," she called unenthusiastically. The woman acknowledged the comment with a wave, then closed the door. Nicole rolled her window back up, folded her arms across her chest and stared straight ahead.

Adam stifled a sigh. Nicole's response had hardly been gracious. But at least she had complied with his instruction. He supposed that was something.

"So why were you late again?" Nicole asked as they made the short drive to the house Adam had purchased the year before.

"A couple of last-minute emergencies came up." Adam had done his best to maintain a more moderate workload than he had in St. Louis, but he still rarely got out of the office before five-thirty or six. "Do you want to stop and pick up dinner at the Bluebird? It's meat loaf night." The Bluebird Café's offerings had become a staple of their diet, and meat loaf was one of Nicole's favorites. Adam's culinary skills were marginal at best, and while he could manage breakfast and lunch, dinner stretched his abilities to the limit. So they frequented the Bluebird or resorted to microwave dinners. Only rarely did he indulge Nicole's preference for fast food.

"Whatever."

He cast a sideways glance in her direction. She was sitting as far away from him as the seat belt would allow, hugging her books to her chest, her posture stiff and unyielding. As distant and unreachable as the stars that were beginning to appear in the night sky. Just like Elaine had been by the time their marriage fell apart four years ago. Now, as then, he felt isolated. And utterly alone. He didn't blame Elaine for his feelings. Or Nicole. His loneliness was a consequence of his own failings. Of his inability to connect emotionally to the people he loved. That was the legacy his own father had left him.

Adam made a quick stop at the Bluebird, and a few minutes later pulled into the detached garage next to his two-story frame house, ending the silent ride home. Nicole got out of the car immediately, leaving him alone in the dark. The savory aroma of their meal filled the car, but even though he'd skipped lunch, he had no appetite. Because he knew what was ahead.

He and Nicole would eat mostly in silence. Any questions he asked would be met with one-word answers. Then she would disappear to her room on the pretense of doing homework. A few minutes later he'd hear the music from a CD. Though they shared a house, they'd each spend the evening alone, in solitary pursuits.

Adam desperately wished he knew how to connect with his daughter, who was as lonely as he was, according to the school counselor. Apparently she'd made virtually no friends in the year they'd been in Hope Creek. *Standoffish* and *prickly* were the words the counselor had used to describe his daughter. At the woman's suggestion, they'd actually gone for a few sessions of joint counseling. But Nicole had been so unresponsive that it had seemed a waste of time.

He rested his forearms on the steering wheel and lowered his forehead to his hands, struggling to ward off the despair that threatened to overwhelm him. And, as always in these dark moments, he turned to God for comfort and assistance.

Dear Lord, I need your help, he prayed silently. *I know I'm not doing a good job as a father. And I know Nicole is unhappy. But I don't know how to get past the wall she's built between us. She hates me, and she shuts me out every time I try to reach out to her. I know I failed with Elaine. I don't want to fail with Nicole, too. Please give me strength to carry on and guidance on how to proceed. I can't do this on my own. I'm so afraid that time is running out for us. I love my daughter, Lord. Please help me find a way to make her understand that before it's too late.*

Slowly Adam raised his head, then tiredly reached for their dinner. But when he stepped into the kitchen a few moments later, Nicole was already nuking a frozen dinner. She turned to him defiantly, daring him to comment.

Adam said nothing. He just set the food he no longer wanted on the table, put her meat loaf in the refrigerator and prepared for another silent, strained dinner.

It was going to be a very long night.

Clare added the column of figures again and frowned. Not good. Even with scrupulous budgeting, six months with no income would be rough. But she could make it. She had to. Because she needed Aunt Jo's legacy.

Clare rose and set a kettle to boil on the stove in her tiny efficiency apartment. She could use the microwave, but she preferred boiling water the old-fashioned way. There was something about a whistling kettle that she found comforting. It brought back happy memories of growing up on the farm in Ohio with her parents and two sisters. Though they hadn't been wealthy in a material sense, they'd been rich in love and faith. It was the kind of family she'd always hoped to create for herself.

And she'd succeeded. Up until two years ago. Then her own selfishness had destroyed both of those precious gifts—faith and family.

Clare swallowed past the sudden lump in her throat. She wasn't going to cry. She didn't believe in such indulgences. She'd made a tragic mistake, and now she'd have to live with the results. Her family was gone. And her faith…it wasn't gone, exactly. It was too deeply ingrained to just disappear. But it had languished to the point that she no longer found any comfort in it or felt any connection to God.

Of course, she still had A.J. and Morgan. She wasn't sure what she would have done without their moral support these past two years. But while they were close emotionally, geographically they were scattered. Besides, her sisters had their own lives, their own challenges to deal with. Clare didn't want to unduly burden them with her problems. Especially her financial ones.

She hadn't communicated the sad state of her finances to Aunt Jo, either. Though she'd written to her great-aunt on a regular basis, she'd always tried to be upbeat. Aunt Jo knew that Clare and Dennis had always lived a good life, enjoying the best of everything. When Clare had moved from a lavish home to an apartment after the accident, she'd simply said she needed a change of scenery. And when she'd reentered the teaching world, she'd explained that she just needed to fill her time. So Aunt Jo had had no idea how precarious her situation was. Otherwise, Clare was sure her aunt would have made some income provision for the six months of the nanny stipulation in her will.

That reminded her—Dr. Wright still hadn't returned her call from yesterday. Clare frowned and glanced again at the figures on the sheet in front of her. It was time for another call to the good doctor.

"Adam, I've got Clare Randall on the phone again. She says it's urgent, and she's willing to hold until you have a few minutes."

Adam stopped writing on the chart in front of him and glanced distractedly at Janice. "Clare Randall?"

"She called yesterday. I left the message on your desk."

Adam frowned. "That was the one marked personal, right?"

"Bingo."

"Do you have any idea who she is?"

"Not a clue."

Adam glanced at his watch. "Do I have a few minutes?"

"Mr. Sanders is in room one, but he's telling Mary Beth about his fishing trip, so I expect he wouldn't mind if you take a couple of minutes. I can't speak for Mary Beth, though. Last time I went by, her eyes were starting to glaze over and she was trying to edge out the door," Janice said with a grin.

Adam chuckled. "You could relieve her."

"No way. Last time he cornered me I had to listen to a twenty-minute soliloquy about the newest hand-tied trout flies he'd discovered."

Adam chuckled again. "Okay. We'll let Mary Beth handle him this time. Go ahead and put the call through."

Adam made a few more notes on the chart, then set it aside as the phone on his desk rang. "This is Adam Wright."

"Dr. Wright, this is Clare Randall. I'm Jo Williams's great-niece. I believe you and my aunt were friends?"

"That's right."

"Well, I'm very sorry to tell you that my aunt passed away two weeks ago."

Adam felt a shock wave pass through him. He and Jo had met at church when he'd first arrived in St. Louis to do his residency, and they'd been friends ever since. Even after his move to North Carolina, they'd kept in touch. In many ways, she had become a mother figure for him, and he had always been grateful for her support and sympathetic ear. He'd had no idea she was even ill. But then, that didn't surprise him. Jo had never been one to burden others with her problems.

"Dr. Wright? Are you still there?"

He cleared his throat, but when he spoke there was a husky quality to his voice. "Yes. I'm just…shocked. I'm so sorry for your loss. Jo was a great lady."

She could hear the emotion in his voice, and her tone softened in response. "Yes, she was."

"What happened?"

She told him of the fast-acting cancer that had taken Jo's life, and then offered her own condolences. It was obvious that Adam Wright had great affection for her aunt. "Did you know her well?"

"We met more than fifteen years ago, and she became a good friend. We attended the same church when I lived in St. Louis. She was a woman of deep faith. And great generosity."

Clare took a deep breath. "As a matter of fact, her generosity is the reason I'm calling you today. As you may know, Aunt Jo didn't have much family. Just me and my two sisters. And she was very generous to us in her will. However, there is a rather unusual stipulation attached to my bequest."

When Clare hesitated, Adam frowned and glanced at his watch. He had no idea what this had to do with him, and he couldn't keep Mr. Sanders waiting much longer. He pulled the man's chart toward him and flipped it open, his attention already shifting to his next patient.

"So how can I be of assistance?" he asked.

"I understand that you have a daughter named Nicole?"

Adam's frown deepened. "Yes. What is this all about, Ms. Randall?"

"In order to claim my bequest, my aunt required that I act as nanny to your daughter for six months, at no charge to you."

There was a momentary pause. "Excuse me?"

Clare's hand tightened on the phone. "I know this sounds crazy, Dr. Wright. Trust me, I was shocked, too."

"But…why would Jo do such a thing?"

"I have no idea."

Adam tried to sort through the information Jo's great-niece had just given him. None of it made any sense—the stipulation, or this woman's willingness to go to such lengths to claim what couldn't be a large bequest. As far as he knew, Jo wasn't a wealthy woman. With her generous heart, she'd given away far more than seemed prudent to him sometimes. But maybe she'd had more assets than he knew.

Adam glanced up to find Mary Beth standing in the doorway. She nodded her head toward room one, pointed at her watch and rolled her eyes. He got the message.

"Look, Ms. Randall, I've got to go. I have patients waiting. Give me your number and I'll get back to you."

Clare did as he asked, then suggested he call Seth Mitchell. "I'm not sure he can explain Aunt Jo's reasoning any better than I can, but at least he can verify that my offer is legitimate," she said.

"Thanks. I'll do that. I'll be back in touch shortly."

When the line went dead, Clare slowly replaced the receiver. Dr. Wright hadn't exactly been receptive to her offer, she reflected. But she couldn't really blame him. She would have reacted the same way. After all, he was a doctor. He probably made more than enough money to hire any nanny he wanted. In fact, he might have one already. So why should he let a woman he didn't know help raise his daughter, even if it was for only six months?

Logically speaking, there were all kinds of reasons why Adam Wright could—maybe even should—turn her down. So she needed to put together a strategy in case he declined to cooperate.

Because Clare needed Aunt Jo's legacy.

And she didn't intend to take no for an answer.

Adam looked across the kitchen table at Nicole. Tonight she was eating the meat loaf he'd brought home last night, while he ate a frozen dinner. As usual, they were out of sync. He speared a forkful of broccoli and searched for something to say, anything that might generate a little conversation.

"So…anything interesting happen at school today?"

She gave him the look he'd come to clearly recognize over the past year. It was a look that let him know how pathetic she thought his overtures were. And even after all these months, it hurt. But he made himself try again.

"Come on, Nicole. Tell me about your day."

With a long-suffering sigh, she lowered her gaze and picked at her food. "There's nothing to tell. It's just a dumb, hick school. Everything and everybody there is boring."

It was the same refrain he'd heard over and over again. So he changed subjects. "I had some bad news today."

She looked over at him. "Yeah?"

"Do you remember Mrs. Williams, from St. Louis? She ran the bookshop and went to our church."

"Yeah. She was nice."

"I found ̤ ̤t today that she passed away a couple of weeks ago."

Nicole looked down at her meat loaf. "Why do people you care about always have to die?"

Adam knew she was thinking of Elaine and the tragic boating accident that had taken her mother's life a little over a year ago. Nicole and Elaine had been close, and though Adam had thought Elaine was too liberal in her child-rearing practices—a frequent point of contention between them—he knew that his wife had deeply loved her daughter. And that Nicole was still grieving for her.

"It was just their time, Nicole," he said gently. "God has His reasons."

"Yeah, well, I don't think God is very nice. He lets bad things happen that just make people sad. I don't know why people are always praying to Him. He never listens anyway."

Adam frowned. Over the past couple of years, he'd been having a harder and harder time getting Nicole to go to church with him on Sunday. And it had become a weekly battle since they had moved to North Carolina. She and Elaine hadn't gone to church regularly, and he knew that the lapse in church attendance had come at a critical stage in Nicole's life, shaking her still-developing faith. It was another change he didn't like in his daughter.

Nicole put her fork down. "May I be excused?"

Adam glanced at her plate. She'd barely touched her food. "Are you feeling all right?"

Nicole glared at him. "Can't you stop being a doctor even for a minute? I feel fine. I'm just not hungry anymore. So may I be excused?"

Adam's gut clenched. His question had been prompted

out of fatherly concern, not medical interest. But clearly Nicole hadn't seen it that way. She saw him as a doctor, not a father. Which only served to underscore the problems in their relationship.

"Yes, you may be excused."

Disheartened, he watched her walk away, then reached into his pocket and pulled out the slip of paper containing Seth Mitchell's phone number. Last night he'd prayed for help with his daughter. Today Clare Randall had called with her offer. That wasn't exactly the kind of help he'd had in mind, but then, God's ways weren't always our ways. Maybe Clare was the answer to his prayer. Since he wasn't getting anywhere with Nicole on his own, and he was rapidly running out of possible babysitters in Hope Creek, he'd be a fool not to at least consider Clare's offer.

He'd been too busy to call Seth Mitchell today. But he'd make that the first order of business tomorrow morning.

Adam slowly replaced the receiver and leaned back thoughtfully in his desk chair. Seth Mitchell had just confirmed Clare's story, though he'd been unable to offer any further insight into Jo's offer. Nor much additional information about Clare herself, except that she was a widow with teaching credentials. When Adam had seemed skeptical about Jo's unusual stipulation, the attorney had assured him that it was completely aboveboard and verified that Clare Randall would expect no payment for her services.

Despite that reassurance, Adam had a hard time accepting the offer. Getting something for nothing was outside the realm of his experience. And it had been ever since he was twelve years old and asked his father for a new bicycle. To this day he vividly recalled his father's gruff response.

"There's no such thing as a free lunch, boy. You have to work for what you want."

So Adam had done just that, doing odd jobs around the neighborhood until he'd earned enough money for his bike. And that was generally the way life had worked for him ever since. Which was why he found it hard to believe that this woman's offer came without any strings attached. Despite what the attorney had said.

Still…he did need help with Nicole. And financially he wasn't in a position to hire a full-time nanny. So wasn't Clare Randall's offer at least worth exploring?

Before he could change his mind, Adam reached for the phone and punched in her number. She answered on the first ring, almost as if she'd been sitting by the phone.

"Ms. Randall? This is Adam Wright. I wanted to follow up on our conversation yesterday. I took your advice and spoke with Seth Mitchell, and he verified that your offer is legitimate."

He paused, and when Clare spoke he could hear the trepidation in her voice. "I sense a 'but' coming," she said cautiously.

"Listen, I'm sorry if I seem a little suspicious, but frankly I keep wondering, what's the catch?"

"What do you mean?"

"Well, if I accept your offer, it will totally disrupt your life for six months. I just can't understand why you'd go through that."

"I'm not going to inherit a million dollars, or anything close to it, if that's what you're asking," Clare said stiffly. "This isn't a TV reality show, Dr. Wright."

She seemed insulted by his question, but Adam didn't

think it was completely out of line. She *was* a total stranger, and he wasn't entirely sure about her motivations. Something just didn't feel quite right to him. Then again, maybe it was his problem, he acknowledged. He was so used to paying his own way that maybe he was just uncomfortable accepting anything as a gift.

"Look, Dr. Wright, would it make you more comfortable if we met face to face?" Clare offered when Adam didn't respond.

He could hear a touch of impatience—or was it desperation?—in her voice. "Maybe," he conceded slowly.

"Then why don't I come down?"

He glanced again at the area code. "Where do you live?"

"Kansas City."

"That's a long trip. And I can't make any promises."

"I'm not asking you to."

If she was willing to make the effort to come down, how could he refuse to meet with her? And what did he have to lose, except an hour or two of his time?

"Okay. Let's try that."

Clare had a couple of substitute teaching assignments to fulfill, so they agreed to meet on a Saturday in mid-November.

"I'll see you then," Clare said as she hung up, already making a mental list of all the things she needed to do to prepare for a six-month absence from Kansas City.

Because even though Adam Wright seemed to have some qualms about accepting her offer, she knew one thing with absolute certainty: One way or another, she would find a way to convince the good doctor that she was exactly what he needed.

Chapter Two

Clare let her car slowly roll to a stop, set the brake and peered through the passenger's-side window at Adam Wright's house. Located at the edge of town, on the side of a hill near the end of a country lane, it was just as he'd described it—a two-story white clapboard with forest-green shutters and a large front porch. It was set on a spacious lot shaded by large trees, and a detached garage was just visible to the right, about fifty feet behind the house. When she turned to look out the driver's-side window, she saw a valley filled with fields and patches of woodland. Blue-hazed mountains were visible in the distance, their wooded slopes ablaze with fall color. It was a lovely, peaceful setting—and completely at odds with her emotional state.

Clare nervously withdrew her compact from her purse and studied her face. Despite her best efforts to artfully apply some blush, she still seemed pale. She also looked tired, but there wasn't much she could do about that. She'd driven straight through from Kansas City, arriving last night about ten. Though she'd been exhausted from the long journey, jitters about today's meeting had kept sleep at bay. She'd tossed and turned most of the night, then risen at dawn in anticipation of her nine o'clock meeting with Dr. Wright. The stress and lack of sleep had clearly taken their toll on her appearance.

After one final, dismayed look, she dropped the compact back in her purse and opened her door. This was as good as it was going to get, she acknowledged with a sigh. Maybe Adam Wright wasn't the observant type, she thought as she made her way toward the front porch.

All such hopes quickly vanished, however, when the front door opened in response to the doorbell. In the seconds before he greeted her, the blue-jean-clad man gave her a swift but thorough perusal that was insightful, assessing—and unnerving. She saw surprise in his eyes—and caution. And even before he said a word, she sensed that something about her appearance had raised a red flag. Nervously she smoothed a nonexistent wrinkle out of her skirt and adjusted the strap on her shoulder purse.

As Adam scrutinized his visitor, he struggled to keep his face impassive. Seth Mitchell had described Clare Randall as a widowed schoolteacher. But the elegant, fashionably clad woman on his doorstep was far from the older, matronly type he'd somehow expected. His prospective nanny couldn't possibly be even forty. And she was small. At five foot ten, he didn't consider himself to be especially tall, but she seemed petite beside him. It wasn't that she was short. She had to be about five foot five. But she was very slender; so slender that the fine, classic bone structure of her face was startlingly evident. She was also lovely. Her honey-gold hair was pulled back into a chignon, and her slightly parted lips looked soft. Despite her beauty, he caught a glimpse of a haunting sadness in the depths of her large, azure-blue eyes that stirred something deep in his heart.

She was dressed beautifully, as well. While he wasn't too knowledgeable about clothes, he did know quality when he saw it. His wife had always bought expensive things, so he recognized the designer touch in Clare Randall's attire. Especially the discreet Gucci logo on her handbag.

The woman obviously had money. Which made her willingness to go along with Jo's stipulation even more suspicious.

While Adam assessed her, Clare looked him over, as well. The doctor appeared to be about forty, with dark-brown hair that was touched with silver at the temples. Even though she wore two-inch heels, he was still several inches taller than her. And obviously in good shape. His worn jeans hugged his lean hips, and his sweatshirt couldn't disguise his broad shoulders or the solid expanse of his chest.

She completed her rapid scan at his eyes. They were deep brown—and they'd narrowed imperceptibly since he'd opened the door. A slight frown had also appeared on his face. Not good signs. Clare felt the knot in her stomach tighten.

"Clare Randall, I presume?" He had a deep, well-modulated voice that Clare would have found appealing under other circumstances. Now she was all too conscious of the subtle note of caution in his tone.

"Yes. Dr. Wright?"

He held out his hand, and Clare's delicate fingers were swallowed in his firm grip. "Guilty. Please come in." He stepped aside for her to enter, then nodded to his right. "We can talk in the living room."

As he led the way, Clare looked around the spacious room with an appreciative eye. It was a lovely space, with high ceilings, tall windows and a large fireplace. It had great possibilities...but unfortunately, none of its potential had been realized. While the living room was meticulously clean, it was sparsely furnished. The leather couch and chair were completely out of sync with the character of the house, and the contemporary coffee table was bare. So were the walls. There were shades at the windows, but no window treatments to soften the austerity.

"Make yourself comfortable."

Adam took the chair as Clare perched on the edge of the couch. From her rigid posture, he could only assume that she was as uncomfortable with this whole situation as he was.

"May I get you some coffee?"

"No, thanks. That's not one of my vices." She tried to smile, but couldn't quite get her stiff lips to cooperate.

Clare's obvious tension reminded Adam of patients with white-coat syndrome. The minute they stepped inside his office their blood pressure skyrocketed and they got the shakes. There was no medical explanation for it. But that didn't make it any less real. Through the years he'd worked hard to put such patients at ease, finding that casual small talk sometimes helped. So it was worth a try with his visitor. He purposely leaned back in his chair and crossed an ankle over a knee, keeping his posture relaxed and open.

"Did you have a good trip?"

"Yes. It took a little longer than I thought, but the scenery is lovely."

"When did you leave?"

"About six yesterday morning."

He frowned. "Did you drive straight through?"

"Yes. As I said, it took a little longer than I thought."

"You must be exhausted."

She shrugged. "I've been more tired."

He studied her for a moment. The light from the window was falling directly on her face, and he could see the faint shadows under her eyes—which he suspected she'd carefully tried to conceal. And despite her obviously fair complexion, she seemed pale.

"Did you have breakfast?"

She shook her head. She'd been way too nervous to face food. "Not yet. I'll get something a little later."

His gaze swept her slender figure. Make that too slender, he corrected himself. "You don't look as though you can afford to skip too many meals, Ms. Randall."

"Please call me Clare. And I've always been slender. But I'm very strong, Doctor, and certainly capable of tackling the nanny job."

He hadn't brought up her weight because of concerns about her capabilities, but clearly the job was on her mind. His attempt at small talk wasn't working. So they might as well dive right in. "First of all, my name is Adam, not Doctor. Second, I have to tell you I've never hired a nanny before."

"And I've never been one. So we're even. But I'm sure I can handle the job. I'm a teacher, so I'm used to being around children."

Adam raked his fingers through his hair and sighed. "Nicole isn't exactly a typical child. My wife, Elaine, and I separated several years ago, and Nicole spent most of her time with her mother. When Elaine died a little over a year ago, Nicole came to live with me full-time. It quickly became apparent to me that she had less-than-desirable friends in St. Louis and seemed to be heading down the wrong path. I'm originally from North Carolina, and I thought moving away from the big city might help. But it hasn't worked out as I'd hoped. She may have had the wrong friends in St. Louis, but she has no friends here. She barely tolerates me. And she hates life in a small town. So she can be very difficult to deal with. Frankly, I haven't been able to keep a sitter for more than a few weeks."

Clare frowned. The situation sounded a lot more complicated than she'd expected. But surely, at age eleven, there was still time for Nicole to turn her life around. "I'm certainly willing to do whatever I can to help."

Adam leaned forward and clasped his hands between his knees. "I guess the real question is why. Why do you want to put yourself into this situation? This isn't a happy household, Clare."

Clare swallowed. It might not be happy, but there was time to make things right. Time for a second chance. Which was something she hadn't had with her own family. Clare realized that Adam was studying her intently, and shifted uncomfortably. This wasn't the time to dwell on the past. She needed to convince Adam that she would make a capable and competent nanny. She took a deep breath and looked back at him.

"I appreciate your honesty. But from everything you've told me, it sounds like you need a nanny even more than you realize," she said.

"Maybe. But you haven't answered my question. Why are you willing to do this?"

"I need the money."

His gaze swept over her attire again, lingering on the

logo on her handbag. When he looked up, she saw the skepticism in his eyes.

"Don't let my clothes fool you, Doctor," she said quietly. "This suit is several years old. The purse is even older. At one time I was in a position to buy expensive things. That's no longer the case. Aunt Jo's legacy will help me pay off some debts and get a new start. And I will do my best to earn it. I promise you that I will do everything I can to help you with your daughter. If it will make you feel more comfortable, I can supply some character references."

Adam studied the woman across from him. He had no reason to doubt Clare's story that she'd fallen on hard times. And as for a character reference, he couldn't ask for anyone better than Jo—the very person who had sent Clare to his door. But the whole thing still struck him as odd. And somehow unfair to the woman across from him. Despite his thumbnail sketch of the situation, she had no idea what a mess she was stepping into. And he had a feeling she'd already seen enough trauma in her life. The echoes of it were still visible in the depths of her eyes. Which, for some odd reason, troubled him, even though she was a stranger.

"That's not necessary," he said. "But I'd like to…"

"Who are you?"

The two adults turned in unison toward the foyer. Nicole stood in the archway at the entrance to the living room, dressed in hip-hugging jeans and an abbreviated crop top. Her brown hair, worn parted in the middle, hung past her shoulders, the ragged blond ends suggesting that it had once been dyed. She was barefoot, and her toenails were painted iridescent purple.

"It's not polite to interrupt a conversation," Adam said with a frown.

Nicole shrugged insolently. "Whatever. We're out of cereal. Again."

The tension between father and daughter was apparent to Clare even in such a short exchange. Before Adam could respond, she smiled and addressed the young girl. "You must be Nicole."

"Yeah. So why are you here? We never have company."

"I had some business to discuss with your father."

"Are you sick or something?"

Clare looked startled for a moment, then grinned. "I'm not a patient, if that's what you mean."

"Too bad. That's the only thing he cares about."

The remark was meant to cut, and if the sudden clenching of muscles in Adam's jaw was any indication, his daughter had hit the mark. But Clare knew it was also a cry for help. And her heart went out to the lonely little girl.

"Oh, I don't know. We weren't discussing medicine," she said, keeping her tone casual.

Nicole tilted her head and gave Clare an appraising glance. "So are you his girlfriend or something?"

"That's enough, Nicole."

Clare could hear anger in Adam's voice. And frustration. Her heart went out to him, too. He was clearly in over his head with Nicole and clueless about how to control a prepubescent daughter.

"Actually, we just met," Clare said mildly.

Nicole studied Clare for a moment. "I like your hair."

"Thanks. But I was just admiring yours. It's so long and full. You could do some really cool things with it."

"Really? Like what?"

Clare considered Nicole for a moment. "Well, I think you'd look terrific in a French braid."

Nicole stuck her hands in her pockets. "I don't know how to do that."

"It's not hard. But it is easier if someone does it for you. Of course, you'd have to even out the ends a little first."

"I haven't cut my hair in a long time," Nicole said skeptically.

"Well, you wouldn't want to lose any length. Just cut it enough to smooth things out." And get rid of the dyed ends, Clare added silently.

"Do you know how to do a French braid?"

"Mm-hm. I used to do them for my sister, A.J., when we were younger. I'm sure there's a salon in town that could do one for you so you could see if you liked it."

"Maybe." Nicole tucked a lock of hair behind one ear. "So...do you live here?"

"No."

"I didn't think so. Everybody here is such a hick. I bet you're from a big city."

"I live in Kansas City now. But I grew up on a farm in Ohio, out in the middle of nowhere. Hope Creek would have been a big city to us," she said with a smile. "What I've found, though, is that most people are pretty nice anywhere you live if you give them a chance."

Nicole grunted. "Not the kids at my school. They all..."

The sudden ringing of the phone interrupted her, and she turned to Adam with a long-suffering sigh. "It's going to be for you."

"Would you grab it and just take a message, please?"

She gave him a hostile look, then disappeared down the hall.

Clare turned to find Adam studying her. "Is something wrong?"

Slowly he shook his head. "I'm just trying to figure out how you managed to do that."

"What?"

"Have a longer conversation with my daughter than I've had in more than a year."

Clare shrugged. "I came without baggage. She obviously resents you, but she doesn't have any feelings for me one way or the other. Sometimes it's easier to talk to strangers."

He dropped his voice. "So what do you think now that you've met her?"

Clare frowned. "She needs friends. And she needs her father."

"The friends part I agree with. The father part… I'm not so sure. She pushes me away every time I try to get close to her."

"She's still grieving for her mother. And dealing with a lot of anger…about a lot of things. She's probably mad at her mother for dying. Maybe she's mad at God. She might be mad at life in general because it seems unfair. You're convenient, so you get the brunt of her anger. And you're an easy target, because you're the authority figure. I'm sure she fights you every step of the way. But you know, even if kids don't like rules, they need them."

Adam sighed. "I guess it helps to have a teaching background. You're probably used to dealing with kids. I never had much…"

"I told you it was for you."

They glanced toward Nicole, who was back in the archway.

"Did you take a message?"

She walked toward Adam and thrust a slip of paper at him. Then she turned to Clare. "So will you be here for a while?"

"At least for a few days."

"Maybe I'll see you again."

"That would be nice."

"Yeah." She shoved her hands in her pockets. "Well. See ya around."

Clare watched Nicole walk away, then looked back toward Adam. He was frowning at the paper in his hand.

"Trouble?" she asked.

He glanced up. "One of my patients. I need to get back to him." He took a deep breath. "You said you planned to be here for a few days?"

Actually, she planned to stay for six months. But she simply nodded in reply.

"Let me sleep on this whole nanny thing, okay? Can I get back to you on Monday?"

"Of course."

"How can I reach you?"

"I'm staying at the Evergreen Motel." She rummaged around in her purse and handed him a card. "You can just call me there."

Adam had driven by the Evergreen Motel many times. It was a nondescript one-story building that had obviously seen better days, on the other side of town. Somehow it didn't fit with this woman's designer clothes and Gucci purse. Nor with the woman herself. Whatever her financial situation now, everything about her spelled class. She was the type who belonged at the Ritz, not the Evergreen.

As he walked Clare to the door and they said their goodbyes, he glanced toward the street. Her car—a modest, older-model compact—was yet another confirmation that she'd fallen on tough times. But why? She didn't strike him as the frivolous type. Was her late husband to blame for her current predicament? he wondered, as she made her way toward the street. If so, he had done a great disservice to his wife. Even after only a brief encounter, he sensed that Clare was a kind, intelligent, empathetic woman, who deserved far more than she currently seemed to have. The thought of her at the Evergreen Motel actually made him feel a bit sick.

Clare reached the car and paused to shift her purse higher on her shoulder, then shaded her eyes with one hand and gazed at the distant mountains. He found himself admiring the natural grace of her movements, as well as her quiet dignity. And he wondered what she was thinking as she looked toward the mist-shrouded peaks.

When she glanced back toward the house, she seemed surprised to find him still standing at the door. And for a moment, he had a sudden, compelling urge to call her back, to offer her a place to stay. Which was very out of character. Because he was not an impulsive guy. And she was a stranger. A moment later, the fleeting impulse disappeared when she slid into the driver's seat.

Adam waited until the car was out of sight, then slowly shut the front door. Even though he'd told Clare he wanted to think about her proposal, he was already pretty sure that he would accept. Because he desperately needed help with Nicole.

And in his heart he had a feeling that Clare was the answer to his prayer.

The water stain on the ceiling in her cramped motel room was the first thing Clare saw when she opened her eyes the next morning, and she quickly averted her gaze. She didn't need luxury, but neither was she used to these kinds of conditions. Tears welled up behind her eyelids, but she refused to give in to them, focusing her thoughts instead on the good, home-cooked meal she'd had yesterday in a quaint little place called the Bluebird Café, and the long, invigorating walk she'd taken through the town. The fresh air, cloudless blue sky and vibrant trees in their autumn finery had done wonders to renew her spirits. She'd arrived back at her room so tired that, despite the lumpy bed, she'd slept soundly. So, physically, she felt better today. And even though Adam hadn't given her a definitive answer to her proposal, she was hopeful that in the end he would say yes.

In the old days, Clare would have taken a moment upon waking to speak to the Lord about her situation. But even though she still tried to pray on occasion, the words were dry and did nothing to quench the thirst in her soul. So her talks with the Lord had become infrequent at best. She wished she had A.J.'s solid faith. Tragedy had only strengthened her sister's relationship with the Lord. Of course, Clare supposed she was better off than Morgan, who seemed to have completely abandoned the faith of her youth in her pursuit of worldly success. Still, Clare felt an emptiness that could only be filled by reconnecting with the Lord. She just didn't know how to go about it.

An image flashed through her mind of the small white church in town that had caught her eye yesterday. Set in a grove of trees, its tall steeple rising toward Heaven, it had called out to her, offering peace and solace. She'd gone so far as to try the door, but of course it was locked in the middle of a Saturday afternoon. However, Clare had made a note of the times for Sunday worship.

She glanced at her watch. If she hurried, she could just make the second service. Since she didn't have anything else planned for the day, and she wasn't inclined to spend any more time than necessary at the Evergreen, she figured it couldn't hurt to go. Maybe worshipping in a new place might give her some fresh insights that would help get her back on track in her faith journey.

When Clare pulled up in front of the church forty-five minutes later, the small lot was already full. By the time she found a parking spot half a block away and stepped inside, the service was just beginning. She had planned to simply slip inconspicuously into a pew in the back, but unfortunately, there were no empty seats in the rear. An usher motioned to her, and before she could decline he was leading the way toward an empty spot near the front. Short of ignoring his hospitality, she had no choice but to follow him.

Clare was aware of the curious glances of the congregation as she traversed the main aisle. She supposed that in a small town like Hope Creek, visitors were big news. But she'd never liked being the center of attention, so she kept her eyes looking straight ahead. Only when she murmured a thank-you to the usher did she glance at the pew across the aisle—and found Adam and Nicole watching her. Adam gave her a brief smile and nod, and Nicole peeked around him and waved. Clare smiled in response, then turned her attention to the service. Or at least tried to. But she found herself casting frequent, surreptitious glances at the doctor and his daughter.

Nicole sat on the other side of Adam, so she couldn't see the young girl very well. But she caught enough glimpses to know that Nicole was dressed in tight black hip-hugger jeans. Her top seemed to be a bit more discreet than the one she'd worn yesterday, but it was not attire Clare would have deemed appropriate for church.

Adam, on the other hand, was well dressed. His broad

shoulders filled out his dark suit, and a gold tie lay against his starched white shirt. He'd looked great yesterday in jeans, and was equally handsome in today's more impressive formal attire, which gave him a distinguished air.

Clare did her best to sing the hymns and listen to the sermon, but the elderly minister was a bit dry, and she found her attention—and her gaze—frequently wandering over to the doctor and his daughter…until she found Adam staring back. For a moment they'd both seemed startled, then Clare quickly looked away as hot color stole on to her cheeks. Served her right, she thought in chagrin. She was in the house of God. That's where her thoughts should be, too. For the rest of the service she made a concerted effort to be more focused.

As the last hymn ended, however, her thoughts returned to Adam and Nicole. She was so preoccupied formulating a greeting in her head that it took her a moment to realize the woman next to her had spoken.

"I'm sorry. Were you speaking to me?"

The older woman smiled at her. "I'm the one who should apologize. You must have been deep in prayer. I'm sorry I interrupted."

Prayer had been the furthest thing from her mind, Clare thought with a pang of guilt. "No reason to apologize. I must admit that I was thinking about something I need to do after the service. But I *should* have been praying."

The woman chuckled. She had short, stylish gray hair that established her senior status, but her blue eyes twinkled with the enthusiasm of a youngster. "That's something we're all guilty of on occasion, I suspect." She held out her hand. "I'm Adele Malone."

Clare returned the woman's firm handshake. "Clare Randall."

"You're new in town."

"A visitor, actually. I'm here on…business."

"Well, I'm glad you joined us this morning. Why, Nicole…"

Clare turned. Adam and Nicole had moved out of their pew, and stood only a few steps away.

"Your hair looks lovely today!" Adele said.

For the first time Clare noticed that Nicole's hair was done in a neat French braid.

"Thank you. It was Clare's idea."

"We had to find a salon that would take Nicole yesterday afternoon without an appointment. But it was worth the effort. The style suits her." Adam's remark was directed at Clare, and she could read the gratitude in his eyes.

Adele looked with interest at Clare, then at Adam. "You two know each other?"

"We just met yesterday. On a business matter," Adam replied.

"How nice. Well, I was just going to invite our visitor to stay and have coffee in the church hall. I hope you can join us, too."

"Not today, I'm afraid. Nicole has quite a bit of homework, and I have to return a couple of pages that I received during the service."

Was there regret in his voice? Or was it just her imagination, Clare wondered.

"Another time, then. I do hope you'll stay, my dear," Adele said, turning back to Clare.

Clare almost refused. But she really didn't have anything else to do today. And if Adele knew Adam, perhaps the woman could offer a few more insights about the good doctor that would help Clare persuade him. "Thank you. I'd like that."

"Good to see you, Adele," Adam said. Then he turned to Clare. "I'll be in touch."

She nodded, and both she and Adele watched as Adam and Nicole made their way out.

"Such a nice man. And a wonderful doctor," Adele said. "Hope Creek was lucky to get him when Doc Evans retired last year. And he certainly tries hard with Nicole. But it's such a challenge raising children these days. Especially alone." She glanced down at the ring on Clare's left hand. "Do you have children, my dear?"

Clare's throat tightened. Maybe someday that question would be easier to answer. But not yet. It still hurt as much as it had two years before. "No. I'm a widow."

The older woman reached over and spoke softly as she touched Clare's hand. "I'm so sorry."

"Thank you."

"I don't suppose that's something one ever gets over. I know I'd be completely lost without my Ralph. He's home today with a cold, and it just didn't feel quite right sitting in church without him. But you have your faith to sustain you. That's such a great blessing in times of trial." She tucked her arm through Clare's. "Now come along and let's get some coffee and a doughnut. Adam's forever after me to lose twenty pounds, but honestly, I don't think one doughnut on Sunday is going to hurt, do you?"

The woman chatted amiably as they made their way to the church hall, where she took pains to introduce Clare to several members of the congregation. It became clear that Adele was quite prominent in the town, obviously active in both church and civic pursuits. When they finally found themselves alone for a moment, Clare glanced at her watch and set down her cup of tea.

"I think I've taken up far too much of your time," she apologized.

"Not at all. I enjoy meeting new people. Will you be in town long?"

"At least for a few days."

"Do you have any friends or family nearby?"

"No."

"So what are your plans for Thanksgiving?"

Clare hadn't really thought much about the holiday, even though it was only four days away. A.J. had just arrived in St. Louis, so she wasn't in a position to leave the bookstore. And the last she'd heard, Morgan intended to work most of the holiday weekend. So Clare had planned to just grab a bite somewhere by herself. Which was a far cry from how she preferred to celebrate holidays, she thought wistfully. Special days should be festive occasions filled with fun and family. But both of those things were now absent from her life. Treating Thanksgiving like any other day seemed the best way to cope without falling apart.

"I really don't have any plans," she told the older woman.

"Then you must join us for dinner."

Clare stared at her, surprised by the impromptu invitation. "But…I wouldn't want to intrude on a family celebration."

Adele waved her concern aside. "You won't be. My husband and I don't have children, or any close family. So we've always invited others to join us for Thanksgiving. The associate pastor and his wife will be there. And Adam and Nicole are coming, too. Adam's only brother lives in Charlotte, and they go to his wife's house for Thanksgiving. So Adam and Nicole will be on their own for the holiday. There will be a few others, as well. You'd be more than welcome."

Clare considered the invitation. It was certainly preferable to eating at the Bluebird, charming as it was. Besides, the café might not even be open on that day. And it would give her a chance to press her case with Adam. But more than anything, she was touched by the older woman's generosity in opening her home to a stranger on a holiday. Her invitation was truly Christian charity in action.

"Thank you," Clare said with a smile. "I'd love to come. May I bring something?"

"Just yourself." Adele opened her handbag and withdrew a small notepad and pen. "I'll jot down my address and phone number. We usually begin to gather about four."

Clare took the slip of paper a moment later and tucked it in her purse. "Thank you, Mrs. Malone."

"Adele, my dear. We aren't that formal in Hope Creek. And it's my pleasure. No one should spend the holiday alone. Or lonely."

As Clare said her goodbyes, she reflected on Adele's parting words. The woman was right, of course. And she'd apparently taken care of the "alone" part for a number of Hope Creek residents. But the loneliness was harder to deal with. Because it went deeper. And wasn't always as visible.

Adam and Nicole came to mind. They lived in the same house. They shared meals. They went to church together. So they weren't alone. Yet Clare knew they were lonely. And sometimes that kind of loneliness was worse than being physically alone. There was something especially tragic about two people living in close proximity who were unable to connect.

Her work would be cut out for her with Nicole, Clare reflected. The young girl desperately needed guidance. But in her mind, there was a whole lot more to this nanny job than simply helping Nicole get her act together.

Bottom line, Adam and Nicole needed to establish a bond. And they needed an intermediary, a catalyst—maybe even a referee—to help them do that.

It would be a challenging role, Clare knew. But she wanted to play it. Because in the short time they'd spent together, she'd felt their pain. And she wanted to help them salvage their relationship before it was too late.

For Nicole's sake, of course.

But also for Nicole's father.

Chapter Three

"Thanks for coming by on such short notice."

Clare nodded. She hadn't expected to hear back from Adam so soon, but when she'd returned to the Evergreen after church and a quick breakfast she'd found a message waiting, asking her to stop by his house at four o'clock that afternoon. She'd called back, confirming the appointment.

"Would you mind if we talked in the kitchen?" Adam asked. "I had to make an emergency run to the grocery store and I just got back. I need to put a few things away."

"Of course."

Clare followed him down a hallway toward the back of the house. At least the sunny kitchen had a little more personality than the living room. It was painted a pale blue, and a border of trailing morning glory vines had been stenciled along the top of the walls. A weathered oak table and four chairs stood beside a bay window that afforded a lovely view of the pine woods on the hillside behind the house.

"Have a seat and I'll be with you in just a minute," Adam said.

She chose a chair that gave her a view of the restful scene out the window. But instead Clare turned her attention to Adam, watching as he rapidly took items out of the plastic grocery bags—eggs, canned soup, bread, lunch meat, crackers, milk, cereal, microwave dinners. She caught a glimpse of his nearly empty refrigerator when he opened the door to put the milk inside.

"Sorry about this," he apologized. "I try not to shop on Sunday, but sometimes the week just gets away from me. Then it becomes an emergency. I thought I'd have everything put away before you got here, but it always takes me longer at the grocery store than I expect."

"Don't worry about it. I didn't have any plans today, anyway."

He glanced at the counter. "I think that takes care of all the perishables. Can I offer you something to drink?"

When she declined, he filled a coffee cup and joined her at the table. "I know I said I'd call you tomorrow, but frankly, I didn't see any reason to wait. Seth Mitchell has confirmed your story. You seem sincere. I trust Jo's judgment, and I desperately need help with Nicole." *And you need Jo's legacy.* He didn't voice that reason. But it had been a definite factor in his decision.

Coils of tension deep in the pit of Clare's stomach began to unwind. "Then you're willing to take me on as nanny?"

He took a sip of his coffee and looked at her steadily. "To be honest, I'm still not entirely comfortable with this. It doesn't seem right for me to accept your services at no cost."

"That was the stipulation in Aunt Jo's will. So there's no choice. And I'm fine with it."

Adam put his mug on the table and wrapped his long,

lean fingers around it. "I talked to Nicole about this. Well, I tried to, anyway," he amended. "I didn't get much more than a few grunts, but at least she didn't throw a fit. So I took that as a good sign. I don't think she'll fight you the way she has every other sitter I hired. But I could be wrong. It could be miserable. For everyone. So what I'd like to propose is that we try this for a month. If everything works out, we can commit to the remaining five months. But this will give us both a chance to test the waters and back out if things don't go well. How does that sound?"

Clare had no intention of backing out. She was determined to make this work. So she had no qualms agreeing to Adam's terms. "It seems like a sensible plan."

"Good. As for your duties, I'm open to suggestions since I've never had a nanny before. I thought you could just make sure Nicole gets ready for school on time so she doesn't miss the bus, and be here when she gets home. During the school day your time would be your own. Nicole could also use some help with her schoolwork. Even though her standardized test scores are always high, her grades have been marginal at best since she came to live with me. With your teaching background, I'd appreciate any help you could provide. Most of your weekends should be free, other than Saturday mornings if I have patients in the hospital and need to do rounds. Ellen James, our housekeeper, comes on Thursdays. She has a key and doesn't need any supervision. Mostly I just need you to keep an eye on Nicole. Does that sound reasonable?"

"Very. And I'll be happy to do some tutoring."

"That would be great. So when can you start?"

"As soon as I find a place to live and get settled in. I hope within a few days."

Suddenly an idea began to take shape in Adam's mind. Considering Clare's current accommodations at the Evergreen Motel, her finances probably wouldn't allow her to upgrade very much when it came to a more permanent place to live. And he had a small, furnished apartment above his garage. Maybe he couldn't pay her, but there was nothing in Jo's will that would prevent her from accepting housing.

"As a matter of fact, I may be able to help," he said. "There's a furnished apartment above my garage that I always planned to fix up and rent out, but I've never gotten around to it. You're welcome to live there. It's the least I can do, considering you're providing your services free of charge."

Clare looked at him in surprise. "Well, that would certainly be convenient." And easy on her tight budget, she silently added.

"Would you like to take a look?"

"Sure."

After retrieving the key from his office, Adam led the way out the back door and down a cobblestone path toward the garage. When they reached the door, his first couple of attempts to pull it open failed. Finally, after he exerted a bit more force, the door swung out.

"I've only been up here a couple of times since I bought the place," he apologized. "The door probably needs to be sanded."

He preceded her up a narrow set of stairs to a small landing where he inserted the key in another door. This one opened easily, and since there wasn't room on the landing for both of them, he stepped inside first. He switched on the harsh overhead light—and immediately regretted his offer.

He'd known the apartment wasn't in great shape, but it was even worse than he remembered. The walls were painted a dingy, muddy beige. The green shag carpeting had seen better days. The garishly upholstered sofa sagged in the middle, and the shade on the lamp beside it was ripped. Even from the front door, he could see that the countertop in the tiny galley kitchen was badly chipped at the edges. A small wooden table and chairs in the tiny eating area were nicked and worn. And he didn't even want to look at the bathroom or bedroom. As near as he could recall, the furnishings in the bedroom included a lumpy bed and a nondescript dresser with a cracked mirror. There was no way he could offer this space to anyone in its present condition. Especially to Clare, with her obvious elegance and breeding.

"Adam?"

He knew he was blocking the door, but he didn't budge. "Listen, this wasn't such a good idea after all. I forgot that this place was in such bad shape."

"Can I at least look around?"

He hesitated. "I'm not sure you want to. This apartment makes the Evergreen Motel look good."

He heard her laugh—a musical sound that he found extraordinarily appealing.

"That bad, huh?"

At least she had a sense of humor. And she was certainly going to need it, considering what she was walking into, literally and figuratively, with him and Nicole. "Let's just say that I think a four-legged creature would be more at home here than a two-legged one."

"Okay, now I *have* to see it."

"Just promise me one thing."

"What?"

"You won't quit before you even start."

She laughed again. "There's no chance of that."

Hands planted on his hips, Adam surveyed the room once more, then shook his head and moved aside. "Okay. But trust me, you won't hurt my feelings if you take one look and run right back down the stairs."

Clare stepped into the apartment, walked slowly to the middle of the room, then pivoted, making every effort to keep her face impassive. Okay, so it was bad. But it was free. And she was pretty handy with a hammer and a paint brush. She completed her perusal of the living room and kitchen area, then peeked into the bathroom. At least it was serviceable. The bedroom, however, didn't fare as well. She would definitely take the lumpy mattress at the Evergreen over this one, which seemed to have a crater in the middle. She returned to the kitchen, opened a few cabinets, checked out the small refrigerator, silent all the while.

Adam watched Clare as she went from room to room, admiring her natural grace even as he berated himself for showing her the apartment. In her slim, black wool skirt and elegant blue silk blouse she looked completely out of place in the run-down apartment. He couldn't possibly let her live here.

"Look, this was a bad idea and I'm sorry for even suggesting it," he apologized as the silence lengthened.

"Actually, this isn't so bad," she said gamely.

He looked at her incredulously. "You've got to be kidding."

"No. I'm serious. Mostly what it needs is a cosmetic makeover. I assume the appliances and heat work?"

"Last time I checked."

She shrugged. "Why don't you let me tackle it? I think I can make this livable."

He raked his fingers through his hair as he skeptically eyed the room again. "I'm not sure it's even salvageable, let alone livable."

"At least let me try."

When he looked into her eyes, he saw determination—and spirit. He suspected she was prepared to argue the case if he withdrew his offer. She must really be strapped for cash if she was willing to take this on, he realized. He thought about just offering to pay for housing somewhere rather than let her deal with this mess, but he knew she'd refuse to take his money. It seemed he'd been backed into a corner. "All right. And I'll send Ellen over to help with the cleaning. But if things don't come together, we'll work something else out, okay?"

"Okay."

"I'll order a new mattress, too. The one in the bedroom seems pretty pathetic."

She looked relieved. "That would be great. Thanks."

"Well, do whatever you need to do. Just save the bills and I'll take care of them. I assume you'll be judicious." He tacked on that last admonition out of habit. He'd always used it with his wife, though it had never worked. That was one of the reasons he hadn't been able to save much money during their marriage. But he was immediately sorry he'd said it to Clare. Luckily, she didn't seem to take offense.

"Of course. I'll get started first thing tomorrow. If all goes well, I should be able to take on my duties as Nicole's nanny in a week. If that's okay."

"Absolutely. I'll have the mattress delivered and the door sanded. Let me know if I can do anything else to help in the meantime."

"Thank you, but I'll be fine. I've gotten used to handling things on my own."

After flipping off the light, Adam followed Clare down the steps. Her head was bent as she navigated the narrow stairs, exposing the delicate nape of her neck below her upswept hair. It made her seem vulnerable. And fragile. And it awakened a protective instinct in him. He recalled experiencing a similar feeling about Elaine early in their marriage. But it had been long absent from his life. Nor did it make any sense now, especially in relation to a virtual stranger who, he suspected, would not appreciate being thought of as either delicate or fragile.

For so many years, the only woman in Adam's life had been Nicole. Worrying about her and their rocky relationship had consumed his thoughts and energies when he was away from work. He'd rarely given any other female more than a passing glance, avoiding well-meant setups by friends and keeping all women at arm's length.

Now Clare would literally be living in his backyard. But as she'd noted moments before, it was a business arrangement, nothing more. And he would do well to remember that. Because even if he was inclined to consider her in a more personal light, that would be a tragic mistake. It was a mistake he'd made once before, with Elaine. And it was one he didn't intend to repeat. It wouldn't be fair to any woman.

Because he just wasn't husband material.

Adam glanced up at Clare's apartment as he hit the electric garage-door opener. As usual, the lights were on. She'd surprised him by moving in right away, even though he'd considered the place unlivable. And no matter what time he looked toward the garage—early in the morning as he grabbed a cup of coffee before leaving for the hospital, or late at night before he went to bed—the lights were on. A pile of debris had begun to accumulate next to the driveway—including the shag carpeting. His work schedule before holidays was always crazy, so he hadn't had a chance to stop in. But he wanted to check on her progress and thank her for assuming some of her duties early. When Clare had found out that Mrs. Scott was going away on vacation during the holiday, she'd offered to watch Nicole after school even though she hadn't officially assumed her position yet.

Adam glanced at his watch. Since Thanksgiving was tomorrow, he'd closed the office early. It was the first time he'd been home before six o'clock in weeks. And there was plenty of time to pay his new nanny a visit before dinner.

The ground-level door to the apartment opened without a problem; the carpenter he'd called had obviously paid a visit. He stepped inside, noting that the stairwell had been cleaned up, as well. The bare light bulbs at the bottom and top of the stairs had been hidden under shades that softly diffused the light. The walls were brighter, too, he noted as he made his ascent. They'd been painted in a soft eggshell color. And the wooden steps had been thoroughly cleaned.

Raising his hand to knock on the door, Adam paused at an unfamiliar sound. His daughter's laughter. His throat tightened with emotion, and he sent a silent prayer of thanks heavenward. He had known it would take a major miracle to get his daughter back on track. But if Clare could get her to laugh, she'd already worked a minor one. He hoped this was just the beginning.

His knock was answered almost immediately, and his words of greeting died on his lips as he stared at the woman looking back at him. Clare's honey-gold hair was carelessly pulled back into a ponytail, and her paint-spattered jeans and sweatshirt were a far cry from her usual designer clothes. She didn't seem to be wearing any makeup, either—unless you counted the specks of paint dotting her porcelain complexion. She looked far younger and less sophisticated than in any of their previous encounters. She also looked very, very appealing.

A faint flush rose on Clare's cheeks, and she dropped her gaze under Adam's close scrutiny. Nervously she wiped her hands on her worn jeans.

"Sorry for the way I look. I wasn't expecting company," she apologized in a breathless voice.

"I didn't mean to barge in. I just wanted to thank you for keeping an eye on Nicole this week. And to see if you needed any help with anything."

She stepped aside and motioned him in. "Actually, everything's going really well. Take a look."

Adam walked into the room, then stopped, stunned by the transformation.

The walls had been painted a sunny yellow. The couch, which seemed to have new cushions, had been slipcovered in a floral print with throw pillows tucked in the corners. A rocking chair had been added, and the ripped lampshade had been replaced. The top of the scarred coffee table was hidden by a large lace doily, and an arrangement of dried flowers stood in the middle. Attractive valances had been draped over the two windows, and the pine floor gleamed under a coat of wax.

Slowly he made his way toward the kitchen area. The blemishes on the wood table and chairs had been masked by bright white paint, and cobalt blue accents on the rungs and table legs added a whimsical touch. Even the nicks in the countertops seemed to have disappeared.

The faint scent of lemon hung in the air, and everything was spotlessly clean.

Adam shook his head and turned to Clare. "This is amazing! How in the world did you manage to do all this in three days?" he asked incredulously.

She grinned, obviously pleased by his reaction. "Lots of elbow grease. I told you I'm stronger than I look. And Ellen was great. Thanks for sending her over. I also had some other help." She nodded toward the bedroom.

He moved toward the doorway. Nicole was on a ladder, sponge painting a wall in peach tones and humming along to some song only she could hear through the earphones of her portable CD player. As she stretched toward the pan of paint, Adam instinctively took a step toward her.

"Be careful, Nicole."

Her placid expression changed to a frown when she saw him. Reluctantly she removed her earphones. "What?"

"I just said to be careful. Ladders can be dangerous."

She rolled her eyes. "I'm eleven. I know how to use a ladder."

"I did the top of the walls already. Nicole's helping me with the rest," Clare said from behind him. "She's doing a terrific job, isn't she?"

Adam turned and looked at Clare. Her eyes seemed to say, "Trust me. I wouldn't let her do anything dangerous. And give her a compliment."

Adam got the message. "This looks great, Nicole." In truth, it did. He really couldn't tell where Clare's handiwork stopped and his daughter's began.

When Nicole didn't respond, Clare glanced at her watch. "Looks like it's almost dinnertime, Nicole. Why don't you clean up in the bathroom, then you can walk back to the house with your dad."

"I'm not finished yet."

"You've already done more than I expected. You were just going to do two walls, remember? You're almost done with the third one. Thanks to you, I'll actually be able to move into the bedroom tonight."

Adam frowned. "Where have you been sleeping?"

"The couch was fine for a couple of nights," she replied lightly. "But I'm anxious to try out the new mattress. It looks very comfortable. Thanks again for ordering it."

"It was the least I could do."

"What do you want me to do with the sponges?" Nicole had climbed off the ladder and now spoke to Clare.

"You can just leave them there. I'm going to do a little more work after you leave. Just show me where you left off."

Adam glanced around the bedroom while Nicole and Clare conferred about the walls. A comforter, still in its plastic bag, stood in the middle of the bed, which had been pulled to the center of the room. The cracked mirror had been replaced with one in a white wicker frame, and a lace runner on the dresser effectively hid the scarred top. Lace curtains hung at the window, and a shade had been added for privacy. As Nicole headed for the bathroom to clean up, Adam turned to Clare.

"Where are you going to put the bed?"

"In the middle, over there," she said, pointing to one of the finished walls. "That way, when I wake up in the morning, I can look out the window and see the fir trees on the hill."

Shrugging out of his jacket, Adam handed it to her. "Hold this for me and I'll move the bed for you."

She took the soft leather garment, which emanated a faint but very masculine scent. "I can do that," she protested.

"It's too heavy for you. This will only take a minute."

Clare thought about arguing, then decided against it. The bed *was* heavy. She'd had a tough time jockeying it to the center of the room so she could paint the walls. And it was even heavier now, with the new mattress on it.

Adam finished the job far faster than she would have. And considering the way his muscles bunched with strain under the fine cotton of his shirt, revealing impressive biceps, she was glad she'd let him handle it.

"Is this about right?" He stepped back to survey his handiwork.

"Perfect."

He slid his arms back into his jacket, then planted his fists on his hips. "Look, Clare, I appreciate all your efforts here. But the nanny position doesn't require heavy manual labor. You could get hurt trying to move something like that bed. Promise me you won't tackle any more jobs like that."

"I think I'm almost done, anyway."

"Promise me."

His deep-brown eyes were intent, and slowly she nodded. "If it's that important to you, okay, I promise. But like I told you, I'm stronger than I look."

Silently he reached for her hand, splaying the small, delicate fingers in his much-larger palm. She was so taken aback that she could only stare, first at her paint-splattered fingers against his strong, yet gentle hand, then into his intense, enigmatic eyes.

"This hand was not made for heavy labor. I'm sorry if you think that's a sexist remark, but it's the truth. You have a very delicate bone structure, and it wouldn't take much to crush these fingers. That's a medical fact, and I don't want to be paying any house calls to my new neighbor. Okay?"

Clare could manage only a one-word response. "Okay."

He held her hand for a moment longer, than slowly released it.

"I'm ready."

With an apparent effort, Adam looked over to his daughter. "I'll be right with you." Then he turned back to Clare. "If you'll give me the receipts for your expenses, I'll write you a check."

She was glad to focus her attention on something besides the quivery feelings that Adam's touch had ignited in her. "They're on the table." She moved toward the kitchen and picked up an envelope, turning to hand it to him as he followed her into the room. "That should be everything. I did an itemized list of the expenses, and the receipts are attached."

Adam withdrew the single sheet of paper, quickly scanned it, then frowned. "This is the total?"

Nervously she brushed back a stray strand of hair that had escaped from her ponytail. "Well, I can pay for the rocking chair if you like. I didn't really need that. And…"

"Whoa!" He held up his hand. "I'm not complaining, Clare. It's far less than I expected. You did all this—" he gestured around the room "—for *this* amount?"

She drew a relieved breath. "Elbow grease doesn't cost much. And I know how to live frugally. You can find some great buys at discount stores," she said with a grin.

Adam glanced again at the sum. His late wife, Elaine, would have spent far more than that on a new handbag. And she wouldn't have been caught dead shopping at discount stores. Nor would she have handled such a reversal of fortune so well.

Clare, on the other hand, seemed to have accepted whatever blow life had dealt her with grace and character. She had obviously once lived a far more luxurious lifestyle, if the Gucci purse and designer clothes were any indication. Yet she had adapted to her reduced financial status. And he hadn't heard her complain once. Not about the Evergreen Motel, nor about the dismal state of this apartment. And there had been plenty to complain about in both cases.

She was a remarkable woman, he acknowledged. And while he'd questioned her physical strength, he had no doubt that she could hold her own with anyone when it came to inner strength.

As they said their goodbyes and Adam followed Nicole down the steps and out into the chilly night air, he glanced back up at the warm glow emanating from the windows of the garage apartment. And he made another surprising discovery.

The warm glow wasn't only in the windows; for the first time in many years, it was also in his heart.

Chapter Four

"Clare's going to Mrs. Malone's tomorrow for dinner, too. Why don't we give her a ride?"

Adam looked up from the file he'd been studying. Nicole hovered in the doorway to his office, hands in her pockets, shoulders tense, her expression defiant—as it always was in his presence. He wished he knew how to make her relax around him, to elicit her laughter, to evoke even a trace of warmth, as Clare had. Already their new nanny had connected with his daughter as he never had. He was glad for Nicole's sake, of course. She needed a friend. But it only made him realize how miserably he had failed.

"You can come in, Nicole," he said gently.

She shrugged. "I have homework to do. I just wanted to ask about Clare."

Since they'd moved to Hope Creek, Adam couldn't recall a single instance when Nicole had come into his office. And she obviously didn't intend to start tonight. But she *had* sought him out and initiated this conversation. He considered that a good sign.

He focused on Nicole's question. Clare's invitation was news to him. But it didn't surprise him. Adele Malone had told him once that no one should be alone on a holiday, and she always made an effort to ensure that everyone within the circle of her acquaintance had a place to spend the day. Obviously the older woman had taken Clare under her wing.

"So can we give her a ride?" Nicole repeated impatiently as the silence lengthened.

Adam couldn't think of a reason to say no. At least not any reason that made sense. There was no way to put into words the vague concern that fluttered along the edges of his consciousness, a subtle caution sign about crossing the line between a professional and personal relationship with his new nanny. He couldn't explain his trepidation to Nicole. Or even to himself. So he was left with no alternative. "Sure. I'll walk over later and ask her."

"I can do it."

"I thought you had homework."

Nicole glared at him. "I can take a break for a couple of minutes."

To talk to Clare, but not to him. The message was clear, even if the words were unspoken. "Okay. Let me know what she says."

A half hour passed before Adam heard the back door slam, signaling Nicole's return. A moment later she appeared at his doorway.

"She said she'd go with us. And to say thanks. Here."

Nicole stepped across the threshhold into his office and set down a plate containing four chocolate chip cookies.

"What's this?"

"Clare made some cookies. I stayed to have a couple. That's why I was gone so long. She asked me to bring you these. I gotta get back to my homework," she said, backing out of the room even as she spoke.

Adam looked down at the homemade cookies, still fresh from the oven, oozing chocolate chips. He reached for one and weighed it in his hand for a moment as the just-baked cookie warmed his palm. Then he closed his eyes and bit into it, letting the sweetness dissolve on his tongue.

It had been a long time since he'd had such a treat. Even though some of his patients had given him homemade cookies last Christmas, he'd been so new to his practice that he'd had no faces to associate with the gifts. But he definitely had a face to associate with these cookies. And more.

As Adam reached for a second cookie, he pictured Clare as he'd seen her earlier in the evening, when he'd stopped in to check on her progress with the apartment. She might be close to forty, but she looked about twenty with her hair pulled back into that ponytail, her face makeup free. Only the sadness that hovered in the depths of her eyes hinted that she'd lived longer than twenty years. Long enough to have experienced—and survived—some terrible tragedy.

Adam hadn't had time to analyze his doubts when Nicole had suggested that they give Clare a ride to Adele's. But now he realized that they stemmed from fear. There was something about Clare that attracted him. Big-time. But it was way too soon for him to have those kind of feelings. He hardly knew her. Besides, she'd come here for one reason and one reason only—to fulfill the stipulation in her aunt's will so that she could claim her inheritance. She had no personal interest in him or Nicole. This was a job. When the six months were over, she'd leave.

In the meantime, he needed to keep his own feelings in check and take pains to encourage nothing more than friendship between them. Because Adam clearly knew his own shortcomings when it came to establishing and maintaining emotional intimacy. He'd failed miserably with both his wife and daughter. He just couldn't give the women in his life what they needed. And he had a feeling that Clare had already experienced enough hurt to last a lifetime. He wasn't going to add to her pain.

Reaching toward the plate, Adam discovered that he'd eaten all four cookies. Clare's gesture had been considerate, and he was touched by her kindness. But he suspected that thinking of others was just part of her nature. As it had been part of Jo's. Though she would only be with them for six months, Adam resolved to savor and appreciate such gestures. Because those small kindnesses, which added so much to life, had been long absent from his.

Adam glanced toward the blue-rimmed crockery dish and suddenly realized something startling. The plate might be empty. But oddly enough, his heart wasn't.

"Reverend Nichols, would you please say the blessing?"

Adele took her seat at the large, lace-covered mahogany table, and the dozen people sitting around it joined hands. Clare reached for Nicole's hand on one side and the young minister's on the other, then bowed her head.

"Lord, we thank You for this food and for the generous hospitality of our hosts, who have taken us into their home for this special holiday. We pray today for those who are not so fortunate, who are experiencing hunger or homelessness or who are alone. We ask You to always help

us follow the example You set, and which our hosts so admirably demonstrate today, of offering the hand of friendship to those most in need. Give us the courage and stamina and grace to do Your work and to follow Your call, wherever that may lead us.

"Finally, Lord, we ask that You give solace to those who are troubled in spirit. As we have been welcomed into this home today, please help those who are lost know that You wait to welcome them, and help them find the path home to You. May they feel Your healing presence and know that even when things seem darkest, they are never alone. Amen."

For a long moment after the prayer ended, Clare kept her head bowed. The young minister's words had touched her deeply. It was almost as if they had been spoken directly to her. She had been feeling spiritually lost for months, going through the motions of her faith, but failing to connect on a deeper level with the Lord. She hoped that Reverend Nichols's prayer would be heard, and answered, for everyone at the table. And she added her own brief silent prayer at the end. *Lord, show me the way back to You.*

When she finally raised her gaze, it collided with Adam's. He was sitting directly across from her, and for the briefest moment, before he shuttered his eyes, there was an odd, unreadable expression in them. Clare sensed that the minister's words had resonated in some way with him, as well. Adam's faith seemed strong, so she doubted that he felt estranged from God. But perhaps the part about being alone had touched him. Because the more she saw of Adam, the more she was convinced that he was deeply lonely. From what Adele had said, he had little family. Just a brother, who was married and lived several hours away. His marriage had fallen apart. His relationship with Nicole was strained and tense. He obviously worked long hours, which probably precluded any sort of social life. When Clare got lonely or needed to hear a friendly, caring voice, at least she could pick up the phone and call A.J. or Morgan. Who did Adam have?

The young minister spoke to her then, and she made an effort to put aside that troubling question about Adam and focus on the conversation. Reverend Nichols kept her engaged in a lively discussion, and she was pleased to discover that he would be taking over as pastor of the congregation when the elderly minister retired at the beginning of the New Year. She didn't discover the answer to her question about Adam, of course. But she suspected she knew it, anyway. Adam didn't have anyone.

And even though she had come into his life on a professional basis, as a nanny for his daughter, for some reason that answer bothered her on a personal level. She didn't know why. And she didn't want to know.

Because she was afraid the answer might scare her.

Something smelled good. Really good.

Adam paused in the mudroom, sniffing appreciatively as his salivary glands went into overdrive. He'd worked through lunch, and he was so hungry that he'd even been looking forward to a microwave dinner. But this didn't smell like any microwave dinner he'd ever eaten.

He shrugged out of his coat and hung it on a peg beside the door, then strode toward the kitchen. When he appeared in the doorway, Clare looked up from setting the table and a slight flush warmed her cheeks. Though her hair was pulled back in its customary chignon, she was dressed casually in jeans and a sweater.

"Hi." Her voice was soft and a bit uncertain.

"Hi." He glanced at the table, which had a large bouquet of chrysanthemums in the middle, then at the stove, where several pots simmered. "What's all this?"

"Dinner."

"I figured that. But cooking isn't in your job description."

She shrugged. "I don't mind. I like to be busy." Which was true. Since the accident, she'd purposely packed her days full so that she had less time for reflection. Besides, nonstop activity helped fill the empty place in her life…though not in her heart or soul, she acknowledged. "I just used what I could find in the pantry and the fridge. But there wasn't much to work with. I hope it's okay."

"If that aroma is any indication, it's more than okay. But I already feel guilty for taking your services as a nanny for free. I don't expect you to cook, too."

"I like to cook. Besides, you'd better reserve your judgment. I haven't spent much time in the kitchen the past couple of years, so I'm afraid my skills are a little rusty."

"Rusty skills are better than no skills, which is what I have," Adam said with a grin.

The corners of her mouth teased up. "I hope you don't eat those words."

"I'd rather eat that food. How did your first day with Nicole go?"

"Fine. I made sure she had something to eat before she left for school, and fixed her a lunch. I was here when she got home, and we worked on her math homework for a while. She's writing an English composition now. I'll work with her a little more after dinner. You can just send her over to the apartment when you're finished."

Adam frowned and glanced toward the table, noting

for the first time that only two places were set. "Aren't you eating with us?"

She shook her head. "I don't want to infringe on your time together."

"Trust me, you're not infringing. Meals are pretty silent affairs around here. Besides, the only way I'll even consider letting you cook for us is if you stay for dinner."

For a moment he thought she was going to argue, but in the end she capitulated. "Okay. Assuming the offer still stands after you've tasted my efforts," she added with a smile. "I'll put everything out while you get Nicole."

By the time he returned, she'd set a third place and arranged the food on the table. There was a large bowl of rice, what appeared to be a chicken stir-fry of some kind, biscuits and a platter of fresh fruit.

"Wow!" Nicole said.

"I second that," Adam added as they took their seats.

Adam gave a brief blessing, and almost before he finished, Nicole was helping herself to a healthy serving of rice. She ate heartily and chatted amiably with Clare, who made a concerted effort to draw Adam into the conversation whenever possible. He appreciated her attempts to include him, but tonight he was content mostly to observe and listen to his daughter's animated voice. For the first time since they'd moved into the house a year ago, their evening meal was something to be enjoyed rather then endured. And he was savoring it. As well as the delicious food. He took two helpings of everything, and Nicole wasn't far behind.

Only later, as Clare rose to clear the table, did he notice that much of her food remained untouched. He also realized that she had grown more subdued as the meal progressed, letting Nicole do most of the talking. And in the brief moment before she turned away, he saw a suspicious glimmer of moisture in her eyes.

Adam had no idea what had distressed her. He thought the dinner had been a great success. He glanced toward the sink and studied Clare's back. For a moment he thought he detected the faintest droop in her shoulders, but even as he watched, she straightened them. And when she turned to put a plate of brownies on the table, her smile was back in place.

"I hope you both left room for dessert."

"Wow!" Nicole said, repeating her earlier comment even as she reached for a brownie. "We never have stuff like this!"

"The meal was delicious, Clare. Thank you."

Short of ignoring his comments, Clare had no choice but to look at Adam. She glued her smile firmly in place, then glanced his way. And almost lost her composure. There was caring and concern and empathy in his eyes. So he'd picked up on her mood after all, despite her best efforts to keep her feelings at bay.

Resolutely, Clare fought down another wave of melancholy. She hadn't expected a simple dinner to affect her so deeply. But as the meal had progressed, she'd felt more and more overwhelmed by the scene, so reminiscent of the family dinners she had once known, filled with laughter and sharing and warmth. It had all served as a stark reminder that those good times were gone forever. Her powerful, painful reaction had thrown her, and long-suppressed emotions had bubbled to the surface. She desperately needed a few minutes alone to regain her equilibrium.

"You're welcome. I'm glad you liked it." She pushed her chair in and reached for the sweater she'd draped behind it. "Whenever you're ready, let me know and we'll go over the English composition," she told Nicole.

"Aren't you going to have a brownie?" Nicole asked, reaching for a second one.

"Not tonight."

She turned to go, but Adam's voice stopped her.

"I'll definitely take you up on your offer of making dinner in the future, assuming you share it with us," he said. "That was the best meal I've had in a long time."

It was too late to take back her offer. But it would be easier next time, Clare consoled herself. She'd be better prepared to deal with the memories—and the regrets. Summoning up a smile, she looked at him. "Thanks. I'll be happy to do it."

"Just get what you need. I have an account at the local grocery store."

"Okay."

Again she turned to go. And again his voice stopped her.

"Clare…is everything all right?"

The caring quality in his voice almost undid her. This time she didn't turn back. "Yes. Everything's fine."

She was lying. He could tell by the slight tremor in her voice. But he had no idea how to help her. With his patients, he could ask them where it hurt, and then use his medical training to fix the problem. But that training did him no good in matters of the heart. Dealing with those kinds of problems required a whole different set of skills, which he was woefully lacking. He'd learned that with Elaine. And Nicole.

The back door closed behind Clare, shutting with a gentle click as she walked into the darkness. Silence fell at the kitchen table as Nicole finished her brownie and then quickly exited, leaving him alone. Yearning for more.

Desperately wishing he knew how to open the shutters on his heart and share the warmth he held inside, instead of always holding back.

Slowly he rose and poured a cup of coffee, then propped his hip against the counter as he took a sip. He heard the door to Nicole's room close, and looked out the window toward Clare's garage apartment. The shades were drawn, masking what was within.

Kind of like the three of us, he thought wistfully.

"Adele, where do you keep the soup containers?" Clare asked.

The older woman bustled over to a large cabinet, opened the door and surveyed the contents with her hands on her hips. "Hmm. They should be in here. Marlene, are we out of those little round containers?"

A middle-aged woman looked up from the cake she was cutting. "I think a new shipment came in. Let me look downstairs."

Adele walked over to where Clare was stirring a large pot of chicken noodle soup. "Smells good."

"Well, I've never cooked in such large quantities before. I hope it tastes okay."

"I'm sure it's fine. And our clients will be grateful. I sometimes wonder what all those people did before we started the Feed the Hungry program."

"How long have you been doing this?"

"Several years. If we can get more volunteers, we might be able to provide a main meal more than two days a week. But people are so busy these days. I'm just glad we recruited you."

Clare shrugged. "My mornings are mostly free. I'm happy to help. It's good work."

"Yes, it is. So how is everything going with the nanny job?"

"Well, it's only been two weeks. But so far, so good."

Adele wiped her hands on her voluminous apron. "That's nice to hear. I'm sure Adam is very grateful to have you. Trying to juggle a demanding career with the challenge of raising a young daughter alone must have been very stressful for him."

"I'm sure it was," Clare agreed as she began ladling the soup into the containers that Marlene set beside her, thinking about the fine lines around Adam's eyes. They spoke of stress and a deep-seated weariness that seemed to reach right into his soul.

"Well, I'm certainly glad he found you," Adele said. "I've already noticed your influence on Nicole's clothes at Sunday services. There have been some subtle changes that are definitely a step in the right direction."

Clare shook her head. "I suspect that balancing my ideas of fashion with Nicole's will be an on ongoing challenge. How to be trendy yet tasteful. I can't believe what young girls wear these days."

"Your work is definitely cut out for you," Adele agreed. "Well, I'm heading out. I have bridge club this afternoon and I have to get ready. Will I see you at church on Sunday?" At Clare's nod, Adele patted her arm. "Good. Don't work too hard, now."

Clare absently stirred the soup as she watched the older woman circle the room, speaking a few words of thanks and encouragement to the other volunteers before she left. She did intend to resume weekly church attendance. Though her faith had been shaken in the past couple of years, and her church attendance had lapsed, she knew deep inside that the core of her faith was still there. She just needed to find her way back to it. One step on that journey was attending Sunday services. And it was an opportunity to support Adam in reinforcing the importance of church attendance with Nicole. Apparently he'd been fighting that battle every week with his daughter. Clare understood his insistence, because the foundation of her own faith had been established in childhood, when weekly church attendance had been mandatory.

She also saw it as another opportunity to act as a mediator between Adam and Nicole. Aside from dinner, it was one of the few occasions during the week when they spent time together. Adam was always gone in the morning before she arrived to get Nicole off to school, and he generally got home just in time for the evening meal. Afterward Nicole retreated to her room while Clare briefed Adam on the day, then he generally disappeared into his office. She did her best to get a conversation going between father and daughter at dinner, and she knew Adam was trying. But Nicole wasn't. So Sunday gave her one more chance to try and make some inroads.

But deep in her heart, she acknowledged that as much as she wanted to bring father and daughter together, attending church with them also gave her one more chance to spend time with the elusive doctor who seemed so alone.

"What's this?" Clare picked up a sheet of paper that Nicole had tossed on the table.

Nicole helped herself to two oatmeal cookies from the new cookie jar on the counter before she answered. "Just a dumb school project. They need volunteers to help. You can throw it away."

Clare scanned the sheet. The class was going to construct gingerbread houses for Christmas, and the teacher was looking for a few people to help coordinate the activity. The sheet was dated the week before, and the activity was in two days.

"This sounds like fun," Clare said. "My mom made a gingerbread house every Christmas, and my sisters and I always helped. Although my mother might have used a different word to describe our contributions, since we ate most of the candy she was planning to use for decorations," she amended with a chuckle. "Don't you want to make one?"

Nicole shrugged. "It sounds like kid stuff."

"Kid stuff is sometimes the most fun. Do they still need help?"

"I guess. The teacher said today she needed a couple more moms."

So Nicole's careless toss of the flyer hadn't been so careless after all.

"Would a nanny do?" Clare asked.

Nicole sent her a cautious look, but Clare could see a glimmer of hope in her eyes. "You don't have to do it. I don't think this kind of stuff is part of your job."

"It can be if I want it to be. I'd like to come, unless you don't want me to."

Nicole chewed on her cookie. "I guess it would be okay. At least I'd have someone to talk to."

Clare took a cookie herself, poured each of them a glass of milk and sat at the table. Despite her careful questions about the social aspect of school, so far she hadn't learned much from Nicole. But the girl seemed more willing to talk today. "Aren't the girls friendly?"

Nicole lifted one shoulder. "They already have their cliques. I don't fit in. But I don't care, anyway."

Her defiant posture was directly at odds with the hurt look in her eyes.

"It's hard to break into an established group," Clare sympathized. "That's true even when you're an adult. When I got married, my husband and I moved to Kansas City. I didn't know a soul. And all the teachers at the school where I taught had worked there for years. I don't think they meant to be unkind, but I still felt like an outsider. I was too new to understand their inside jokes, and a lot of them were single and hung out with each other after work while I went home to my husband. It took me quite a while to feel at home there."

Nicole eased into the chair next to Clare. "So did you do something to…you know, make them like you?"

"Well, it's hard to *make* people like you," Clare said gently. "But most of the time, if you let people get to know you, then they decide on their own to like you. I finally figured that out, after about three months. So I made it a point to ask them questions about their lives, and to tell them about mine. Then I invited all the teachers to our house for a barbecue."

"Did they come?"

"Mmm-hmm. And after that, things got a lot better."

Nicole frowned and played with the crumbs of the cookie that had fallen on the table. "The girls at school think I'm a snob."

"Why would they think that?"

Spots of color appeared on Nicole's cheeks and she kept her eyes downcast. "I might have called them hicks once."

"I can see where that could be a problem. I'm sure that hurt their feelings."

"Yeah."

The disheartened tone of Nicole's voice tugged at Clare's heart, and she reached over and took the young girl's hand. "But I bet there's a way to make things right."

"Yeah?" Nicole looked up hopefully.

"Let me think about it, okay? And in the meantime, how about we make some gingerbread houses?"

Nicole was right. The girls in her class did snub her. Most of the time she was alone, her shoulders stiff and hunched, her back to the rest of her classmates as she worked on her gingerbread house. Clare's heart went out to her. She knew the girl desperately wanted to make friends, but her body language said Keep Out—a message the rest of the class definitely heeded. The other girls were clustered in small groups, giggling and laughing as they admired each other's handiwork, oblivious to Nicole's misery—or just ignoring it.

It didn't take Clare long to pinpoint a blond-haired girl named Candace as one of the class leaders. She flitted from group to group, a born organizer and trendsetter. Many of the girls seemed to take their cues from her. So that was where she needed to start, Clare decided. She picked up the paper containers of candy she'd parceled out for decorations and slowly made her way toward Candace, giving out candy as she went. When she reached the blond-haired girl, she paused and smiled at Candace's creation.

"That looks great!" Clare said. "I like how you used the peppermints for stepping stones."

The girl turned to her and giggled. "Thanks. But I think I ate too many of them. See, I ran out." She pointed to the abrupt end of the path.

"Well, we can fix that." Clare took a paper cup with

several peppermints in it and set it beside Candace. "There's even a couple extra if you're still hungry," she said with a wink.

"Great!" Candace glanced toward Nicole, then gave Clare a curious look. "So are you really her nanny?"

"Yes."

"That must be hard."

"Why?"

Candace shrugged. "Nicole's kind of…well, prickly, you know? She always seems mad. Nobody likes her."

"That's too bad. She's had a really hard time, so she could use some friends."

After strategically placing a gumdrop on her house, Candace turned to her inquisitively. "What do you mean?"

"Well, her mom and dad got divorced a few years ago, and she lived with her mother. Then her mom was killed in an accident just before last Christmas. I bet it was a really sad holiday for her." Clare paused and glanced toward Nicole, then looked back at Candace. "Anyway, after that she went to live with her dad. But he decided to move here, so she had to leave all her friends behind. That's an awful lot of stuff to deal with. Enough to make anybody mad, don't you think? And sad, too."

Candace frowned and looked uncertainly toward Nicole. "Yeah, I guess so."

"So what are you going to do with your gingerbread house?" Clare asked.

Candace continued to look at Nicole, and when she spoke her voice was more subdued. "I'm going to give it to my mom for Christmas."

"Well, I'm sure she'll like it very much. I'm going to check and see how Nicole is doing on hers, but let me know if you need any more candy, okay?"

"Yeah, thanks."

Clare made her way toward Nicole, sending Candace a surreptitious glance as she admired her charge's handiwork. The other girl was still watching them, a troubled expression on her face.

Mission accomplished, Clare thought.

Chapter Five

"I thought I'd decorate the house tomorrow. Where do you keep your Christmas things?" Clare asked as she sliced a carrot cake for dessert.

Adam's face went from placid to troubled at the question. Other than an artificial tree, he didn't have any holiday decorations. Elaine had always handled the decorating, and she'd taken all the expensive goo-gaws with her when they'd separated. He'd never bothered to replace them. It didn't make much sense to waste a lot of time decorating when he'd lived alone and spent most of his time at the office, anyway. Then when Nicole had come to live with him shortly before the holidays last year, he'd had other things on his mind. Now, in retrospect, he realized that he should have made more of an effort to celebrate the holiday. Their Christmas last year had been a pretty dismal affair. He had tried to roast a turkey breast so they had some semblance of a holiday meal, but it had come out dry and overcooked. In the end, he'd sent for pizza from a local joint that was the only place open.

"Adam?" Clare prodded when he didn't respond.

"We don't have any," Nicole said, shooting Adam a resentful look. "Except for a dumb fake tree that's in the basement."

His neck reddened at his daughter's indictment, and Adam expected to see censure in Clare's eyes, as well. But when he finally had the courage to look at her, there was only sympathy and compassion reflected in their deep-blue depths.

"Well, I think we can fix that. Assuming your dad agrees."

"Absolutely," he concurred. "Get whatever you think we need."

"How about you and I go shopping on Saturday?" Clare said to Nicole.

"Cool!"

"And I definitely think we should have a real tree," Clare added, a plan taking shape in her mind. "There's an Elks lot at the edge of town that seems to have a good selection. And I saw in the paper that there's going to be a holiday festival downtown on Sunday, with carolers and roasted chestnuts and all the trimmings. What do you think, Adam?"

She supposed she should have discussed it first with him privately, in case he didn't like the idea. But Clare didn't want to give him the option of saying no. He and Nicole needed to spend time together in family activities or they'd never develop any kind of rapport. Fortunately, he didn't seem to object.

"That sounds good. In fact, let's make a whole day of it. We can stop after church and have breakfast, then we'll come home and change before we head out to pick a tree."

Nicole eyed him warily. "You never do stuff like that."

He gazed at her steadily. "Maybe it's time I started."

Nicole didn't respond. But before she turned her attention to the generous wedge of carrot cake that Clare placed before her, Adam saw the barest flicker of something in her eyes. Something he couldn't quite identify, but for a brief moment, it seemed a little bit like hope.

When he looked over to Clare, he saw different messages in her eyes. Approval. Gratitude. And something more. Something even less identifiable than the emotion in his daughter's eyes. But just as potent.

With a hand that wasn't quite steady, Adam picked up his coffee cup and took a sip as Clare reached down to place his cake in front of him. And as her arm brushed his shoulder and her faint, pleasing scent invaded his nostrils, he suddenly felt warm.

And it wasn't from the coffee.

They had shopped till they were ready to drop. Or at least Clare was ready to drop. Nicole seemed to have plenty of energy left, Clare thought with a wry grin as she watched her young charge veer off to check out yet another clothing display.

They'd finished their shopping for affordable decorations at the Wal-Mart on the edge of town, then Clare had suggested they head for the nearest mall—which, much to her surprise, turned out to be nearly thirty miles away, just outside of Asheville—on the pretense of helping Nicole find a Christmas present for her father. But Clare's real agenda was broader than that. She also wanted to supplement Nicole's wardrobe with a few more age-appropriate items of clothing. She'd discussed it with Adam, and he had totally agreed that Nicole's clothing left something to be desired. But he'd had no clue how to guide her.

So he'd basically ended up letting her buy whatever she wanted, only to disapprove of it when he actually saw it on her. Clare hoped to begin rectifying that situation today.

"Ooh, look at this cool top!" Nicole called, holding up an orange knit sweater that looked as if it had shrunk.

Clare tried not to shudder as she pictured it on Nicole—skin-tight and midriff baring. But she knew that if she wanted to make any inroads on the youngster's taste she needed to temper her response and use as much tact as she could muster.

Clare joined Nicole and reached out to finger the top. "I like the material," she said, keeping her tone conversational. Then she tilted her head and studied Nicole's face. "I'm not sure about the color, though. You have such beautiful deep-green eyes…let's see." She glanced around the junior department, then walked over to a display table and selected a longer crew-neck cotton sweater in forest green. "Take a look at this, just for the color," she said, positioning Nicole in front of a convenient mirror and holding the garment in front of her. The shade of green was almost a perfect match for the girl's eyes, and the effect was startling. Her French braid highlighted the developing classic bone structure of her face, and the sweater put the focus on her best asset—her large green eyes.

"Wow!" Nicole said.

"Yeah. Wow!" Clare agreed with a grin.

Nicole studied her image, then frowned as she fingered the sweater. "Too bad it's so long."

"I don't think it will look quite as long when it's on," Clare said. "Why don't you try it? And it would look great with a pair of black pants. Let's see what we can find."

Half an hour later, they left the store with not only the

sweater and black pants, but a modestly short plaid skirt and black turtleneck. As well as a tie for Adam.

"Do you think my dad will mind that we bought all these clothes?" Nicole asked anxiously as they made their way toward the car.

"No. He said it was okay if you got a few new things," Clare assured her.

"It's really different than the stuff I usually buy."

"But you like it, don't you?"

"Yeah. A lot. It kind of makes me think of some of the clothes you wear." Clare was saved from having to think up a response by Nicole's next comment. "You should have gotten something for yourself."

Clare smiled. "I have enough clothes."

"But you wear the same stuff a lot."

Clare couldn't deny that. She'd left some of her clothes in storage in Kansas City, but she'd disposed of much of her wardrobe at a resale shop when she'd moved into her apartment. Dennis had frequently encouraged her to buy new things, and she'd done so because it seemed to please him. But her interest in clothes had been marginal at best, and it had completely waned with his death. So she'd kept some of the more classic, well-made things that would wear well and stay in style, and gotten rid of the rest. Besides, her new lifestyle didn't call for designer suits and cocktail dresses. And the money she'd made from her closet purge had come in handy.

Clare turned to Nicole and grinned. "Are you saying my wardrobe is boring?" she teased.

Nicole smiled in response. "No. I like what you wear. But new clothes are fun."

"And just where would I store them? Have you seen

the closet in my apartment? It was made for a Barbie doll."

Nicole giggled. "It is pretty small."

"That's the understatement of the year," Clare said wryly as they stowed their packages in the car and settled in for the drive home. "It's a good thing I left some of my clothes in Kansas City."

"So were you always a teacher when you lived there?" Nicole asked.

For the briefest second Clare's hand froze as she fit the car key in the ignition. "No. For a while after I got married I taught, but then for a long time I didn't work outside the home." She put the car into gear and began to back out of the parking spot.

"How come?"

Clare swallowed. It wasn't that she purposely kept her past a secret. But it was so hard to talk about. And there'd been no reason to bring it up. Until now. "I—I had a baby. And I decided to stay home with him."

Nicole's head swiveled toward her and her eyes grew wide. "Wow! I didn't know you had a baby! You never told me that. Where is he?"

"He died."

There was a long moment of silence, and when Nicole spoke again her voice was more subdued. "Dad told me that your husband died. He didn't tell me about your baby."

"He doesn't know. I don't talk about it much."

"Why not?"

Because it was my fault. And the guilt overwhelms me when I think about, Clare silently cried. But her spoken words were different. "It still…hurts too much."

Nicole turned to look out the front windshield. "Yeah.

I know what you mean. I still miss my mom a lot. It's like I still kind of expect her to come back, you know? Because she wasn't sick or anything. She just went out on a boat with her friends and I never saw her again."

"That's the same way it happened for me. Only it was a car accident."

"How old was your baby?"

"He wasn't a baby anymore then. He was eight."

"What was his name?"

"David."

Silence filled the car as Nicole digested that. "It must have been really hard for you to lose two people you love. I just lost one. And at least I still had my father, even though he isn't very good at being a dad. Did you have anybody?"

"I had my sisters."

"But they didn't live near you, did they?"

"No."

Nicole sighed. "That's hard. It's like, with my dad, even though I don't talk that much to him, at least I know he's around. That helps a little, you know? But I still get lonesome sometimes."

"I'm sure your dad feels the same way."

"I don't know," she said skeptically. "He's always so busy, I don't think he has time to be lonesome."

Clare thought about the helpless, hungry look she'd seen in Adam's eyes when he watched his daughter. He desperately wanted…needed…her affection. And she thought about the other look she'd sometimes seen when he thought no one was watching, a look that spoke of deep, soul-wrenching loneliness.

"You might be surprised. Some people just hide their loneliness very well," Clare said softly.

"Are you lonely?"

"Sometimes."

"So what do you do?"

"Find something to keep me busy. Or maybe talk to God."

"Yeah. I tried that, too. But He doesn't listen."

"How do you know?"

"Because nothing ever changes."

Clare was still trying to think of a response when Nicole spoke again, this time more thoughtfully. "Well, maybe that's not really true."

Clare sent her a quick, curious glance. "What do you mean?"

"Things did change when you came. I told God that I hated my new life, and I asked Him to fix it. I wanted Him to make my dad move back to St. Louis, so I could be with my friends again. I asked and asked for a long time, but when nothing ever happened I finally figured praying was a waste of time. So I quit. But maybe He was listening. Maybe instead of making Dad move back to St. Louis, He sent me you instead."

Nicole's insight jolted Clare. She'd often learned from her students, and today was certainly no exception. Clare thought about her own sporadic prayers, and how she'd felt much the same way as Nicole—unheard and desolate. The only difference was that Nicole had had hope when she prayed. Clare, on the other hand, had known all along that there was no way God could fix the mess she'd created for herself. Her prayers had been a nebulous plea born of desperation for something…mercy, peace of mind, strength, forgiveness. She'd never put a name to her request. And she'd never felt it had been answered.

But maybe Nicole was right. Maybe God had heard

her. Maybe Aunt Jo's legacy was the answer to her prayer. Maybe, with Nicole and Adam, He was giving her an opportunity to redeem her mistake by putting her in a position to help another family get the second chance her own would never have.

It certainly wasn't the answer she'd expected. Or wanted.

But it *was* an answer.

And a challenge.

Because even though she felt she'd made some progress with Nicole, and laid some groundwork to strengthen the relationship between father and daughter, she knew there was still a whole lot of work to do before those two lonely people could be called a family.

"What do you think, Nicole?"

Nicole studied the tree that Adam was propping up for their inspection and gave a nod of approval. "It's perfect."

"Mission accomplished," Clare pronounced.

"Good! I don't know about you ladies, but my fingers are starting to turn numb," Adam said with a relieved grin as he signaled to one of the attendants on the lot and handed over the Fraser fir for bundling. "How about we go get some hot chocolate?"

"Sounds great to me," Clare agreed.

Nicole chatted excitedly with Clare as they drove back into town, and even included Adam briefly in the conversation.

"So can we put the tree up when we get home?" she asked him.

"Sure."

"Clare and I got some stuff for it. Bows and tinsel and lights and glass ornaments. You can help us decorate it, if you want."

Adam felt his throat tighten, and when he spoke his voice was a bit rough at the edges. "I'd like that."

A short time later he pulled into a parking spot in the town square and they piled out of the car. A few snowflakes had begun to drift down lazily, and the crowd—or what passed for a crowd in Hope Creek—seemed to be in good cheer as residents ambled around, stopping to sample cookies and hot cider at the shops of the various merchants who were taking part in the festival. Carolers sang in the gazebo in the middle of the square, accompanied by a local brass band.

Adam glanced at Nicole. She seemed totally caught up in the festive scene, and her eyes were shining. He smiled and turned to Clare. She looked especially lovely today, he realized, as he tried to swallow past the sudden lump in his throat. Her dark-blue earmuffs and matching scarf brought out the azure color of her eyes. A few delicate snowflakes clung to her golden hair, and her cheeks were flushed from the cold. Her breath came out in frosty clouds through softly parted lips.

Adam felt his pulse begin to pound. He'd glanced her way to see if she'd noticed Nicole's good spirits. Instead, he'd noticed her.

Clare wasn't sure what to make of the expression on Adam's face. It had started off as merely friendly, and she'd been prepared to respond in the same way. But it had rapidly changed to something intense and more than a little unnerving. She felt her heart stop, then race on, as the warmth in his eyes enveloped her. It wasn't the kind of warmth produced by a blazing fire that boldly vanquishes everything in its path. It was more like the deeply buried, white-hot heat of a smoldering ember just waiting for the right moment, the right circumstance, to ignite it.

"Hi, Nicole."

With a supreme effort, Clare looked away from Adam and glanced down. Candace was standing a few feet in front of them with a couple of other girls. Nicole seemed so taken aback by her classmate's greeting that it took her a moment to find her voice.

"Hi."

"Is that your tree?" Candace pointed to the car behind them.

"Yeah."

"It looks nice. We got ours last week."

"We're going to decorate it later. We just stopped to get some hot chocolate."

"Ben's has a stand over by the gazebo. They have awesome hot chocolate."

"Okay. Thanks."

"See you Monday."

"Yeah. See you Monday."

Nicole watched the girls walk away, then looked up at Clare with an awed expression. "Candace stopped to talk to me," she said in a hushed voice.

"I noticed."

"She's never done that before."

Clare put her arm around Nicole's shoulder. "Maybe she's had a change of heart."

Her face alight with hope, Nicole looked back at the girls, who were quickly disappearing among the other holiday revelers. "Yeah."

Adam watched the exchange, knowing he was missing something significant. But the nuances were lost on him. He doubted they were lost on Clare, however. So he'd just have to rely on her to fill him in later.

As they made their way toward the gazebo, it suddenly occurred to him that he was beginning to rely on

Clare for a lot of things. Which wasn't necessarily good. He was immensely grateful for the small but important changes that she had already brought to their lives, of course. But he needed to remember that this was not a permanent arrangement. Clare would be with them for six months. Actually, closer to five now. He had spoken about the time limit of the arrangement with Nicole when he'd told her about Clare's offer, but he needed to remind her periodically so she didn't become too attached. Otherwise, Clare's departure at the end of May would be devastating.

And he needed to remind himself, as well, he acknowledged. Or he had a feeling that Nicole wouldn't be the only one who was devastated.

"Now I remember why I hate tinsel," Adam grumbled good-naturedly as he draped a few more strands over a sturdy branch of the Fraser fir.

"Stop complaining," Clare chided with a smile. "Tinsel is what makes a tree magic. A tree without tinsel is like…like a hot fudge sundae without the hot fudge."

"We never had tinsel," Nicole offered. "And Mom and I never decorated ourselves. Some people always came and did it for us. Our tree looked different every year, too. One Christmas it was all white."

Clare couldn't imagine having a totally different tree every year, but she kept her thoughts to herself. For her, Christmas was all about tradition. About taking out treasured ornaments and sharing memories of where and when they'd been acquired, and about the warmth and caring and laughter of family holiday rituals.

"So did you always have a real tree?" Nicole interrupted her thoughts.

"Absolutely."

"I'm going to grab some cookies. Anybody want some?" Adam asked.

"You're just trying to escape the tinsel job," Clare accused with a smile.

"Guilty as charged," Adam admitted with a grin.

"I'll take a couple," Nicole told him.

"Clare?"

"None for me, thanks."

"And did you always have tinsel?" Nicole asked, resuming the previous conversation.

"Always."

"Did David help you decorate?"

At the sound of shattering glass, Adam sharply turned from the doorway. Clare had dropped one of the round glass ornaments on the hardwood floor and it lay broken at her feet. She stared down at it, her face suddenly pale.

Nicole moved beside her and gently touched her arm. "I'm sorry, Clare," she said contritely.

Adam watched as Clare struggled to compose her features, noting the tremor in her hand as she put her arm around Nicole's shoulder. "It's okay. Just chalk it up to my clumsiness."

Hardly, Adam thought. *Clumsy* and *Clare* were not words anyone would ever use in the same sentence. Nicole's question had obviously upset Clare deeply. Unfortunately, Adam hadn't really been listening very closely to the exchange as he headed for the kitchen. He thought his daughter had mentioned someone named David. But Adam was pretty sure that Seth Mitchell had told him Clare's husband's name was Dennis. So who was David?

Adam didn't have a clue. But Nicole obviously did. And he intended to get the answer to his question at the earliest opportunity.

"That was another great meal, Clare. Thank you."

"I'm glad you liked it." She smiled, but some of the light had faded from her eyes since they'd decorated the tree earlier in the afternoon.

"You look a little tired. Why don't you let Nicole and me handle the dishes tonight."

Nicole looked at him in surprise. "You never help with the dishes."

"You're right. And I'm wrong. The cook shouldn't also have to do the dishes."

"Really, Adam, you don't have to do that," Clare protested. "You work all day. And you're tired when you get home. I don't mind."

"I didn't work today. And I'm not tired tonight. You, on the other hand, look like you need some rest. Go climb into a hot tub with a good book or a cup of tea. Doctor's orders."

She managed a tired grin. "The hot tub part sounds good, anyway. Are you sure you don't mind? Just for tonight?"

Her quick capitulation told him more eloquently than words that his assessment had been correct. But he suspected Clare's exhaustion was more emotional than physical. "Not in the least." He rose and began clearing the table as if to demonstrate his point.

"Well…okay. Nicole, don't forget to finish that reading assignment tonight."

She groaned. "Do I have to?"

"Absolutely. Promise me you'll do it."

"Okay, okay. I promise," she grumbled.

Clare glanced at Adam as she passed and nodded toward Nicole.

"I'll make sure she finishes it," he said quietly.

He waited until the door shut behind Clare before he turned to Nicole. "How about you scrape the plates and put them in the dishwasher and I'll work on the pots?"

She hung back warily. "I have to finish my homework."

"It can wait a few minutes. Or I could see if Clare would come back and help. But she looks pretty tired."

His ploy worked. "I'll help."

They worked in silence for a few minutes as Adam struggled to find a way to broach the subject of David.

"The tree looks nice," he said.

"Yeah."

Silence.

"Did you have much luck on your shopping trip yesterday?" he tried again.

"Yeah."

More silence.

He closed his eyes and took a deep breath. Why wasn't there a book on how to talk to teenage daughters? None of his medical texts had ever addressed this issue.

"So did you and Clare buy some clothes?"

"I did. Clare didn't."

"Why not?"

"She said she has enough."

"Well, maybe she does."

Nicole gave him an exasperated look. "Don't you notice anything? She always wears the same stuff."

Adam couldn't argue with Nicole, because he really

didn't pay that much attention to what Clare wore. He just knew that she always looked good.

"So are we going to get her a Christmas present?" Nicole asked when he didn't respond.

Adam looked at her in surprise. "Do you think we should?"

Nicole gave a long-suffering sigh. "Of course. You're supposed to give stuff to people you like. And she probably won't get anything else, except maybe from her sisters."

"Okay. What do you think we should get?"

"Clothes."

That seemed a little too personal. "I don't know. How about a cookbook?"

"Good grief, Dad. You are so out of it!"

"What's wrong with a cookbook?"

"She already knows how to cook. Real good, too. If you give her a cookbook, she might think you don't like her cooking."

He frowned. That certainly wasn't his intent. But now that Nicole had pointed it out, he could see how the gift might be misinterpreted. "You may have a point," he conceded. "So what kind of clothes did you have in mind?"

"I saw her looking at this pretty blue sweater with beading around the top at the mall in Asheville. I think she really liked it, but it was kind of expensive."

A sweater. That didn't seem too personal. So it would probably be safe. "That sounds like a good idea. Do you want to go with me to get it some night this week?"

Nicole hesitated, and he held his breath. He knew she was debating the torture of spending time with him against the desire to do something nice for Clare.

"Okay, I guess," she said slowly. Then she sighed and

went back to stacking plates in the dishwasher. "Maybe that will help me make up for upsetting her today."

Bingo. That was the opening he'd been waiting for.

"I heard her drop the ornament. What happened?" Adam kept his voice casual and continued scrubbing a pot.

Nicole paused and stuck her hands in her pockets, her face troubled. "I shouldn't have brought up David. I think she misses him a lot."

"Who's David?"

"Her son. He died in the car crash with her husband."

Adam's hands stilled, and he sucked in a sharp breath. He'd had no idea! When Seth Mitchell had mentioned that she was a widow, the man had made no reference to a double tragedy that had taken both her husband and son. Now he understood the source of the ever-present pain in Clare's eyes.

"I hope she's not mad at me."

Nicole's comment brought him back to the present, and he turned to his daughter. "She knows you didn't mean to make her feel bad. Sometimes it's just hard to be reminded of people you love when they're gone. It takes a long time to stop missing them."

Nicole's face grew sad. "Maybe you never do."

He knew she was thinking of her mother. "Maybe not," he conceded. "But it does get easier in time."

Her shoulders hunched and she dropped her head. "Yeah. I guess. But you don't miss Mom like I do."

Adam dried his hands on a dish towel and reached out tentatively to lay a hand on her stiff shoulder. He was afraid she'd pull away, but she didn't. "Your mom and I had some good times, Nicole," he said gently. "I like to remember those. And I miss them. But I wasn't the best husband. I was too caught up in my work. And I've never been very good at letting people know what's in my heart. I have a lot of regrets about the way things turned out between your mom and me. But at least one good thing came from our marriage. You."

Nicole looked up at him, and he saw a glimmer of unshed tears in her eyes. "Sometimes I feel like I just get in your way," she said in a choked voice. "Like you'd rather talk to sick people than to me."

His gut clenched, and his instinct was to reach out and pull her close. But he was afraid she'd back off. So he restrained the impulse. "That's not true. It's just easier to talk to them sometimes because I can usually help them solve their problems. But I've never been very good at solving problems for the people I love. I can't write a prescription for those."

She studied his face. "You don't always have to fix everything. Sometimes just listening is enough."

He tried to swallow past the lump that suddenly appeared in his throat. "I'll remember that."

They looked at each other for a moment, then Nicole backed up a step. Adam let his hand drop to his side. "Well, I gotta go finish my reading." She glanced around the kitchen. "Are we done?"

"Yeah. I think so."

As he watched her leave, he realized that this was the longest civil conversation he'd had with his daughter since she'd come to live with him. And he also realized his response to her last question hadn't been quite accurate.

Because he had a feeling they weren't done. They were just beginning.

And his heart felt lighter than it had in a long time.

Chapter Six

"Okay, she's almost done in the kitchen. Should I bring it out now?"

At the sound of the excited, low-pitched voice behind him, Adam turned from the crackling fire and nodded at Nicole. "I think it's time."

As his daughter scampered away, he thought back to their outing to the mall in Asheville. Though they'd spent much of the time in silence, and their conversation had been mostly strained, there had been a few occasions when they'd seemed to connect. Those fleeting moments had given him hope that their relationship might be turning a corner. As far as he was concerned, that was the best present he could have received this holiday season. And it was thanks to Clare.

Adam leaned back in his chair and slowly looked around the living room. Spruce garlands, held in place with festive plaid bows, were draped on the mantel, around the doorways and on the stair rail in the foyer. Strategically placed white twinkle lights added magic to the setting. Sparkly snowflakes of all sizes and a collection of pine cones were displayed on the mantle, interspersed with glowing candles of varying heights. A feeling of warmth and peace enveloped the living room. And he had Clare to thank for that, too.

As well as for the early holiday meal they'd just shared. Roast lamb, new potatoes and a spinach soufflé that melted in their mouths. Not to mention the fabulous chocolate mousse. And all of it had been homemade. Tonight's hearty, delectable fare had been a far cry from the sparse, sometimes unidentifiable nouvelle cuisine and imported chocolates, fine wines and designer pastries that had been staples of the catered holiday dinners Elaine had insisted on during most of their marriage. Those meals had been stiff and formal. Tonight's had been homey and relaxing.

It had also been unlike anything he'd known as a child. Their Christmases had always been rather sober; the meals quiet affairs served by a succession of equally dour housekeepers. Tonight had reminded him of what he'd missed…and what he still yearned for.

Nicole reappeared then, diverting his thoughts. As she tucked a beribboned package under the tree, Clare appeared in the doorway carrying two presents of her own.

"Well, it looks like we all had the same idea," she said with a smile as she made her way to the tree and placed her gifts beneath the scented boughs.

It hadn't occurred to Adam that Clare would have gifts for them, as well, and he was doubly grateful for Nicole's suggestion. His daughter gave him a smug I-told-you-so look when he glanced at her, and he responded with a grin and a thumbs-up signal.

"Open ours first, Clare," Nicole instructed.

Clare flushed and sat cross-legged on the floor, then reached for the foil-wrapped box. "I didn't expect this."

"We wanted to do it. Didn't we, Dad?" Nicole prodded.

"Absolutely."

Clare tore the wrappings away, then lifted the blue, pearl-beaded cashmere sweater from the tissue. Her eyes widened, and she looked first to Adam, then to Nicole. "This is the one we saw in Asheville."

"Nicole said you admired it."

"Yes, I did, but…it's way too generous."

"So do you like it?" Nicole chimed in excitedly.

"I love it. Thank you." She ran her hands gently over the whisper-soft wool, then looked at them curiously. "Did you go together to get this?"

"Of course. Sending me to the women's clothing department with only a description would have been a recipe for disaster," Adam said with a chuckle.

"I had to show him the way," Nicole chimed in. "He almost got lost trying to find the right department, and the sweater was in a different place than when we looked at it. He would never have found it by himself."

"Well, it's a good thing you went, then."

"It was a very successful outing," Adam said. Clare saw the deeper meaning in his eyes and smiled in response.

"So can I open my present now?" Nicole asked excitedly.

"Of course. But I'm afraid mine aren't as grand as the one you gave me," Clare said as she handed Nicole a package.

The young girl quickly tore open the wrappings, then lifted out a knitted angora cap that matched her new green sweater.

"Ooh, this is awesome!" She jumped to her feet and

tugged it on, then examined her reflection in the mirror over the mantel.

"I'm so glad it fits!" Clare said in relief. "The pattern was a little vague on sizes, and I couldn't exactly ask you to try it on without ruining the surprise."

"Did you make this?" Nicole asked in awe.

"Mmm-hmm."

"Way cool!" The girl admired her reflection for a moment longer, than turned to Adam. "Aren't you going to open yours?"

Clare reached for the remaining box and silently handed it to Adam. He pried the tape off and carefully eased the box out of the wrapping, then lifted the lid. Nestled in the folds of the tissue was a gray-and-black knitted tweed muffler of fine wool.

"You made this, too?" At her nod, he looked down again and fingered the subtle herringbone pattern. He couldn't remember the last time anyone had given him such a thoughtful gift, one that clearly represented a significant investment of time. His throat tightened, and he took a steadying breath. "It's wonderful. Thank you, Clare."

A warm flush suffused her face. "You're welcome."

He examined the scarf more closely, then shook his head. "This looks complicated. So does Nicole's. When in the world did you find time to make them?"

She shrugged. Sometimes, when the nights seemed especially long, occupying her fingers—and her mind—helped pass the dark hours and kept unhappy thoughts at bay. "Here and there," she said lightly.

"I'm going to wear mine to Uncle Jack's," Nicole declared.

"What time are you leaving tomorrow?" Clare asked

as she began to gather up the remnants of their early Christmas exchange.

"Right after breakfast. We should get to Charlotte by noon if all goes well. What time will your sister arrive?"

Clare was looking forward to A.J.'s visit more than she could say. She was just sorry that Morgan had been unable to get away from work long enough to make a trip south more practical. "Sometime tomorrow. It depends on how early she can leave. I wish she could stay longer, but at least we'll have three days."

"She's in St. Louis, right?"

"Yes."

"That's a long drive for just a three-day visit."

"She won't mind," Clare said with a chuckle. "She likes to travel. I think *Adventure* is her middle name."

Adam grinned. "Well, I'm glad you'll have some company while we're gone. But I'll leave the phone number in the kitchen, just in case you need to reach me. Though you'll probably be glad to have us out of your hair for a few days."

His comment was made in jest, but in fact, Clare knew she would miss the Wrights.

Both of them.

She kept that thought to herself, however, and responded instead with just a smile. Because that seemed a whole lot safer than giving voice to what was in her heart.

"Hey, bro, are you gonna share some of the couch or not?"

From his prone position, Adam opened one eye and looked up at his younger brother. "Not."

"Then I might just have to sit on top of you."

Adam groaned. "Have some mercy. I can't move after that enormous meal. How do you stay in such good shape, eating like that all the time?"

"I don't eat like that all the time. Usually we just nuke a microwave dinner."

"Jack!" His wife poked his arm playfully as she came up behind him.

He gave her a saucy grin and looped his arms around her waist. "Hey, I'm not complaining. I didn't marry you to cook. You excel at…other things."

Theresa's face turned bright red. "You are incorrigible."

"But you wouldn't have me any other way, would you?" he said cajolingly as he kissed her cheek.

She squirmed out of his embrace and turned to Adam. "I want you to know that we do not have microwave food every night. With two kids…" she paused and gave her husband a wry look, "…make that three… I try to prepare healthy, homemade meals most of the time."

Adam chuckled. "Don't worry, Theresa. I only believe half of what Jack says. If that much."

Jack planted his fists on his hips and feigned a hurt look. "I don't know if I can take all this abuse. First my wife, now my brother. And on Christmas, no less."

"Get out the violins," Adam said wryly.

"Well, you do have some redeeming qualities," Theresa conceded. "You always remember to take the trash out, and you did stay up until two in the morning last night putting together Bobby's new bike."

Jack grinned and draped his arm around his wife's shoulders. "That's not a bad start on an apology. But we'll work on a better one later." He winked playfully.

She rolled her eyes and shook her head, but her smile was affectionate. "Like I said…incorrigible."

"So how about a turkey sandwich?" Jack said innocently.

Theresa stared at him incredulously. "We just finished the dishes!"

"I hear some turkey calling my name."

"It takes one to know one," she replied pertly.

"Ooh, low blow!" Jack said with a chuckle. "Never marry a woman who talks back, Adam."

Adam smiled. "You're lucky Theresa puts up with you."

"Isn't he, though?" Theresa concurred with a grin.

Jack reached for her hand and pulled her close. "Yeah, I am," he said, his eyes suddenly serious. "Merry Christmas, Mrs. Wright." He leaned down and brushed his lips over hers.

The spell was broken a moment later when a loud crash sounded from the far reaches of the house. Theresa sighed and extricated herself from her husband's embrace. "Sounds like a new toy has bitten the dust already. I'll take care of it. You two need some guy-time to catch up."

Adam watched her leave, envying the easy give-and-take between husband and wife. It was something he'd yearned for, but had never found with Elaine.

"What's with the look?" Jack asked as he sank into an overstuffed chair beside the couch.

Adam turned toward him and shrugged. "You seem to have it all."

Jack laughed. "Yeah. Mortgages and sibling fights and a never-ending list of chores. Plus a boss who drives me nuts."

"Not to mention a wife who loves you completely and makes all those everyday problems seem incidental."

Jack cocked his head and eyed Adam speculatively. "Hey! Are you coveting Theresa?" he teased.

Adam smiled, but his voice was weary. "Maybe. Are any of her sisters still single? And good with kids?"

Jack's face grew more serious. "Still having trouble with Nicole, huh?"

"That's putting it mildly."

"Teenagers are tough. I'm not looking forward to that stage, either."

"At least you've got Theresa to help. With that and other things. I have to admit I am a little envious, Jack." He sighed, and when he spoke again his voice was quiet. "To be honest, I...I never had anything with Elaine that came close to what you have with Theresa."

"Elaine was...different," Jack said carefully.

"What do you mean?"

Leaning back, Jack stretched his legs out in front of him and jammed his hands into his pockets. "She wasn't the warmest person I ever met," he said slowly. "I don't mean to speak ill of the dead, but honestly, Adam, I never could figure out what you saw in her."

In retrospect, Adam had to admit, he couldn't, either.

"She was very beautiful," Adam offered.

"True. But that's not enough to keep a relationship going for the long-term."

"Jack? Can you come in here for a minute?"

Theresa's voice interrupted them, and Jack gave Adam an apologetic look. "Don't move. I'll be right back."

Adam watched as Jack exited the room, then sat up and leaned forward, resting his forearms on his thighs and clasping his hands as he gazed at the flickering flames in the fireplace. Jack was right about Elaine's beauty, of course. But the physical chemistry that had initially drawn him and Elaine together had been powerful. Powerful enough to sustain their marriage long after it should have ended. And powerful enough to undermine his good judgment at first.

He thought back to their courtship. Things had moved quickly. Too quickly, he acknowledged. Always an introvert, Adam had been so flattered that someone like Elaine, so vibrant and beautiful, would take an interest in him, that he'd proposed far too soon. He knew now that the proposal had been prompted by her complaint that the demands of his residency hadn't given them enough time to spend together. He hadn't wanted to lose her, and he'd figured that a proposal would demonstrate his serious intent. Once they were engaged, she'd been so caught up in the flurry of wedding plans that his preoccupation with his work had no longer been an issue. Still, her displeasure should have warned him of stormy seas ahead. Because doctors were often as busy, if not more so, than residents. As his practice had grown, Elaine had come to hate the demands of his job, which often pulled him away from home at odd hours or made him miss social events. Soon she spent more and more time shopping and socializing with friends to compensate for his lack of attention and had run up bills that began to alarm Adam. By the end of their marriage, they'd been deeply in debt. It had taken him years to regain financial stability.

As their marriage had deteriorated, Adam had begun to wonder what Elaine had seen in him. Gradually he'd come to believe she had been more attracted to the notion of being married to a doctor than of being married to him. It gave her a certain prestige and cachet with her friends. That had been a hard pill to swallow. And it had made him even more withdrawn.

Adam leaned back and wearily closed his eyes. He knew there were a lot of reasons for the breakup of their marriage. Basic incompatibility, for one. They'd had different interests and tastes and priorities—which would have surfaced if they'd taken more time to get to know each other before rushing into marriage. Elaine's insistence that they remain in St. Louis after Adam's residency, despite his intention to return to North Carolina, had also led to resentment on both sides.

He knew they both shared the blame for the disintegration of their marriage. But he was painfully aware of his part in it. Especially his inability to allow people to get close to him. That had eventually alienated Elaine. It continued to hinder his ability to establish a rapport with his daughter. And it made him afraid to even consider a future romantic relationship. He knew that unless he found a way to unlock his heart, he was destined to remain alone—and lonely—for the rest of his life. Which was a really depressing thought for Christmas Day.

"Sorry about that." Jack dropped back into his chair. "Minor crisis in the bedroom. Bobby's foot got stuck under the dresser."

"Is he okay?"

"Yeah. This kind of stuff happens ten times a day. So where were we? Oh, yeah. You were coveting my wife."

Adam smiled. "Not really. I'm happy you found Theresa. I just wish I knew how you…" He raked his fingers through his hair. "I don't know. You two have such an easy give-and-take. Like you're always on the same wavelength at some really deep level." He shook his head in frustration. "I don't know how to explain it. Or how you do it. I wish I did."

Jack shrugged. "There isn't really a secret. You just

share things. Make sure the other person always knows how you feel about stuff."

Adam sighed. "You make it sound so easy."

"It is."

"Not for me."

"You're just different than me, Adam. You know, the still-waters-run-deep thing. A lot goes on under the surface. It doesn't mean you feel any less than I do. I'm just more up-front with my emotions."

"I wish I was." Adam clasped his hands together and looked down. There was silence for a moment, and when he spoke again his voice was halting and laced with pain. "Sometimes I think I'm becoming just like Dad."

"No way!" Jack exploded, his voice fierce as he leaned forward intently. "Don't ever think that! Dad was a bitter, resentful, unkind man who was incapable of expressing love. I'm not even sure he knew what love was. If I didn't dislike him so much, I'd feel sorry for him. I used to wonder what made him the way he was. But frankly, at this point I don't even care anymore. God forgive me, but I'm glad he's gone so my children won't be exposed to him. You are nothing like him, Adam. Nothing!"

Adam searched Jack's eyes. He wanted to believe his brother. But his fears ran deep. "Even if you're right, I'm just as bad as he was about expressing emotions."

Jack studied him. "Okay, so maybe you need a little work in that area. But the thing is, at least you feel them. He didn't. You're a kind, compassionate person. He wasn't. I'm just sorry for what he did to you. For making you feel so awkward and uncomfortable about showing affection. For making you so afraid to let people get close."

"But you lived there, too. You don't have the same problems. Maybe it's me, not him."

"Uh-uh. Don't buy it. I just have a different temperament. The old man and I clashed all the time because I never cared about winning his approval the way you did. I realized early on that it was a lost cause. That's why I joined the navy when I was eighteen—to put as much distance between me and him as possible. And I never looked back."

Adam leaned back and expelled a long breath. "You were smart."

"So are you. The first step toward fixing a problem is recognizing it. You've done that."

"Yeah. But I still don't seem to be making much headway with Nicole. I just don't know how to reach her."

"She has other problems, Adam. She just lost her mom. She's in a new town. She had to leave all her friends behind. She's probably mad at life in general. That's a lot of stuff to deal with. It's not just you."

"That's what Clare says."

"The new nanny?"

"Yeah."

"Well, she's right. But if it's any consolation, I think Nicole's far less prickly now than when we visited you last summer. And the relationship between the two of you seems to be a little more cordial. That's a step in the right direction."

"I hope so. But I can't really take the credit for any positive changes. Clare's had a lot of influence on her."

"Then three cheers for Clare! And you want to know something else? I think maybe she's had a positive influence on you, too."

"What do you mean?"

"Do you realize that this is the first time in our lives that you actually opened up and shared your feelings with me? I'd say that's cause for celebration. And if Clare's the reason, more power to her. In fact, let's drink an eggnog to that."

He stood, but Adam put a hand out to restrain him. "I appreciate the sentiment, but I don't like eggnog."

Jack leaned down and spoke in a conspiratorial whisper. "I'm not crazy about it, either. But Theresa says it's a holiday tradition and she won't be happy until it's all gone. So play along, okay?"

He returned a minute later with two large glasses. "How about we go out on the deck for some fresh air and have our eggnog," he said in a louder-than-normal voice.

"Sure," Adam replied with a grin.

They shrugged on their coats, and once they stepped out on the deck, Jack quickly dumped the eggnog behind a convenient bush. "Whew! Safe for another year," he said with a mock sigh of relief. Then he withdrew two cans of soda from under his jacket and handed one to Adam. "Better?"

"Much."

They popped the tops, and Jack's face grew serious as he held his can up in a toast. "To all the things that really matter. And to Clare…may she continue to fish in still waters."

Adam looked at Jack in surprise. That wasn't his brother's typical irreverent toast. But as he lifted his can, Adam couldn't think of anything he'd rather drink to.

"Okay, enough about the bookshop and the ongoing saga with my partner, Mr. Conventional. Tell me about you."

Clare grinned at A.J. Her sister had spent the last hour regaling her with hilarious tales of her escapades in Aunt Jo's bookshop, from her drowned-rat arrival in the midst of a rainstorm to the apparent chaos she was wreaking on the peace of mind of her partner, Blake, who was having a hard time coping with A.J.'s many changes to the shop. Clare hadn't laughed so much in years.

"I'm afraid my story isn't nearly as entertaining," she apologized.

"Well, lay it on me anyway. I take it you don't have to fight the good doctor every step of the way like I do my nemesis?"

"No. I think he knew he was in over his head with his daughter and that he needed help. So he's pretty much given me free rein with her."

"Excellent. And how's the problem child doing?"

"Coming around, I think. But it'll take time. She's had a lot of stuff to deal with." Clare gave A.J. a quick recap.

When she finished, A.J. frowned. "Wow! That's tough. Losing your mom, being uprooted, leaving your friends behind. No wonder she got off track."

"And, of course, Adam bears the brunt of her anger. He tries to reach out to her, but she backs off. I know that hurts him. I can see it in his eyes. Bottom line, I think they're both very lonely people who are hungry for affection and love but who live very isolated lives. Nicole is beginning to blossom, though. She just needed some nurturing and some guidance. I'm not sure what it will take to get through to Adam, though."

A.J. eyed her speculatively. "But that's not your problem, anyway, is it? You're just supposed to be a nanny for Nicole. There wasn't anything in the will about her father."

Clare stared at the miniature tree in her tiny apartment. "True. But I'd like to help them both if I could. The opportunity to create a family is such a precious gift. I'd hate to see them throw it away."

Clare's voice broke on the last word, and A.J. reached over and squeezed her hand. "I know how hard this must be for you, Clare," she murmured.

There was silence for a moment. Then Clare took a deep breath and turned to her sister. "It will be better after the holidays are over. It's just that so many of the things I did with Nicole and Adam this year made me remember the good times with Dennis and David. We had wonderful Christmases, A.J. I want Nicole and Adam to have the same thing. For a lot longer than I did."

A.J. nodded. "I understand. And I know you'll do your best to make that happen."

Clare did, too. But she didn't know if her best would be good enough to heal the immense rift that threatened to keep father and daughter from ever becoming a real family.

Clare frowned at the columns of figures in front of her. Her financial situation was precarious at best. And today it had taken a turn for the worse. Of all the rotten times to need a root canal! Even though that tooth had been damaged in a sledding accident more than twenty-five years ago, it had never given her a bit of trouble. Until now. So much for the slight cushion her rent-free situation had provided. Her dental bills were going to wipe it out. But given the pain in her tooth, she didn't have much choice. What a belated Christmas present!

A knock sounded at her door, and she looked up distractedly. Except for Nicole and, on rare occasion, Adam, she never had visitors. Especially in the middle of the day. Curious, she rose and moved toward the door. When she pulled it open, she was startled to discover Adam on the other side.

"Is everything all right?" she asked in alarm.

"I was just about to ask you the same thing."

She stared at him blankly, still trying to process his uncharacteristic midday appearance at her door. "Your tooth?" he prompted, when the silence lengthened.

"Oh! Right. My tooth. Is that why you stopped by?"

A faint flush crept up his neck. "I was on my way from the hospital to my office and had to swing by here to pick something up. I thought I'd drop in and see what Mark had to say."

Clare had been reluctant to incur the expense of a dentist visit, but when her distress had been evident at dinner last evening, Adam had insisted on calling Mark Miller, a dentist friend in Asheville. He'd arranged for Clare to see him this morning.

"Oh. Well, come in for a minute. It's cold in the hallway." She moved farther into the room, and after a brief hesitation, Adam followed. "Have you had lunch?"

"Not yet."

"I'm just heating some soup. Would you like some?"

Another brief hesitation. "Don't go to any trouble. I can only stay a few minutes."

"It's no trouble, and the soup is almost ready."

"Okay. Thanks."

"Have a seat at the table." She preceded him, and he caught a glimpse of columns of numbers on the sheets of paper she quickly gathered up as she cleared a place for him.

"So tell me about the tooth," he said as he shrugged out of his leather jacket.

She made a wry face. "Not good. I need a root canal."

He grimaced. "Ouch."

"Yeah." In more ways than one, she thought as she stowed her budget scribblings inside a drawer in the kitchen.

"When is he going to do it?"

"Friday. I figured that would give me the weekend to recover in case there are any aftereffects."

Adam frowned. "Don't wait on our account. If you need to take a day or so off, we can cope."

"I'll be fine." She ladled the soup into two bowls and put them on the table, along with a basket of crackers and a plate of cookies. "I'm afraid this isn't a very substantial lunch," she apologized.

"It's more than I often have," he assured her. "Things get pretty crazy at the office and a lot of times I just skip lunch. I'm glad I didn't today, though. This is delicious," he said appreciatively as he sampled the hearty beef barley mixture.

"I like soup for lunch in the winter. It's not hard to make, and one pot lasts me all week."

He stopped eating long enough to look at her. "You made this?"

"Mmm-hmm."

"My compliments to the chef."

She inclined her head. "Thank you."

As Adam wolfed down his soup, he realized that Clare was hardly making a dent in hers. She was eating each spoonful gingerly, taking care to avoid the tooth that needed work. "Are you sure you can wait till Friday?" he asked with a frown. "I could call Mark and ask him to fit you in sooner."

She looked up from her bowl. "No. I'm just being careful. But don't feel like you have to stay until I'm finished. I'm sure you're in a hurry."

Adam glanced at his watch. If he left immediately he'd barely get to the office in time for his first appointment. Which was his own fault. He'd only intended to make a quick inquiry, then be on his way. But Clare's unexpected invitation had been too tempting to turn down. He rarely saw her alone, and the opportunity to spend a few minutes with her had been immensely appealing.

Adam wasn't really sure why he'd detoured to the house at all. He certainly could have done without the file he'd retrieved from his home office. And a simple phone call would have sufficed to alleviate any concern he had about her dental problem. His impromptu visit had been impulsive and completely out of character, he acknowledged.

He looked over at Clare, noticing for the first time that she was wearing the blue sweater he and Nicole had given her for Christmas. He suddenly realized that it matched her expressive eyes exactly. His gaze dropped to her soft lips, lingered a moment too long, then returned to her eyes. And for just a moment he got lost in their azure depths. Lost enough to experience a brief moment of panic.

"I'm used to eating alone, Adam. So please don't stay on my account," Clare repeated, her voice now a bit breathless. "I can see you're concerned about being late."

In an abrupt move that momentarily startled her, he reached for his jacket, said his goodbyes and quickly made his escape.

Because suddenly he was concerned about far more than being late.

Chapter Seven

The midwinter cookout was a smashing success.

Clare breathed a sigh of relief as she watched the giggling clusters of girls roasting hot dogs around the bonfire, noting with satisfaction that Nicole was firmly ensconced in the middle of one of them. Since she'd run into Candace at the Christmas festival in town, Nicole had seemed much happier. She talked about school more, and it sounded as if the girls had begun to include her in their activities. So Clare had thought a party might give Nicole another helping hand. She'd made it a point to talk to each of the mothers in advance, hoping to ensure good attendance, and her efforts had obviously paid off.

"Looks like they're having fun, doesn't it?"

Clare turned. Adam stood just behind her, holding the oversize thermos of hot chocolate he'd retrieved from the kitchen. She smiled and looked back at the group of girls. "I'd say so. It brings back memories of good times as a kid, doesn't it?"

When Adam didn't respond, she turned back to him. He had an odd expression on his face, one that she couldn't quite identify. Instinctively she reached out to touch his arm. "What is it, Adam?" she asked softly.

For a moment he didn't answer. Then he looked down at her gloved hand, which rested lightly on the sleeve of his sheepskin-lined jacket. A different expression flitted across his eyes, and she saw his Adam's apple bob. A moment later, he nodded toward the thermos. "Where do you want this?"

He was ignoring her question. Which was certainly his right, since she'd trespassed on to personal ground. She should just let it go. But something compelled her to persist. "Adam, what's wrong?" she tried again.

Reluctantly he raised his gaze to hers, as if he were afraid to let her see his eyes. But they were shuttered now, anyway. "Nothing."

She replayed their conversation in her mind, wondering what she'd said to trigger his look. Then she briefly glanced back toward the bonfire. "This doesn't bring back happy memories for you, does it?"

A muscle clenched in his jaw, and she was pretty sure he was going to ignore her question. But he surprised her by answering. "It doesn't bring back memories of any kind," he said flatly.

She frowned. "What do you mean?"

"I didn't have the best childhood, Clare. Nothing like the one you described at Christmas. My mother died when I was six. I barely remember her. My father was a good provider, but he wasn't exactly…demonstrative. He was a hard taskmaster who expected his sons to toe the line and not be distracted by frivolous things. We never had parties like this."

Clare's eyes softened with empathy. She couldn't even imagine a childhood like the one Adam described, devoid of love and laughter. Suddenly a few more pieces of this man's life clicked into place. How could you connect to people you love if you had no experience with love yourself, no example to follow? "I'm sorry, Adam. That wouldn't have been an easy way to grow up."

He shrugged stiffly. "It could have been worse. We always had a roof over our heads and we never went hungry."

Maybe not for food, Clare thought. But his youthful diet sounded sadly lacking in emotional sustenance.

"So where do you want this?" he repeated.

She pointed toward a long table set back from the bonfire. "Anywhere over there is fine. Thank you."

As she watched him walk away, his back ramrod straight, Clare's heart ached for him. No wonder he'd had difficulty sustaining a marriage and bonding with his daughter. Being raised in a strict, emotionally cold environment would have left him ill-equipped for either task. Yet she knew that Adam craved emotional closeness. She could see the longing, as well as the discouragement, in his eyes when he looked at Nicole. He was obviously convinced that he didn't have the tools to create the kind of bond he yearned for with his daughter.

But Clare was sure he was wrong. Because she'd seen something else in his eyes, as well. A fire burning deep in their depths. A capacity to love just waiting for release. A hunger to connect. She believed with all her heart that he desperately wanted to escape the loneliness that he thought was his destiny, to fill the emotional vacuum created by his sterile upbringing.

And she also believed that where there was a will, there was a way.

It might be one of the biggest challenges of her life,

but Clare was determined to help Adam find the key that would unlock his heart so that he and Nicole could finally become a family.

Clare was freezing.

As she groggily came awake, she automatically reached for the fluffy comforter, only to realize it was already covering her. She frowned and peered at the illuminated face of her clock. Two in the morning.

Shivering, she reached for her bedside lamp and flipped it on, blinking as light flooded the room. Something was wrong with the heat, she realized, as a frosty cloud of breath suddenly appeared in front of her.

Clare didn't have a clue about the heat source for her apartment. Adam had shown her how to work the thermostat when she'd moved in, and she'd never had a need to investigate further. So she had no idea how to fix the problem. She couldn't bother Adam at this hour, but she had to do something. Even if she piled every blanket in the apartment on her bed, it wouldn't be enough to keep her warm.

Taking a deep breath, she forced herself to get up. With shaking fingers she rummaged in the dresser for her heavy wool sweater and pulled it on over her nightgown. Then she slipped her arms into her velour robe. Finally, after wrapping the comforter around her shoulders, she padded out to the living room to examine the thermostat.

It didn't surprise her to find that the temperature in the apartment was thirty-nine degrees. So her next stop was the furnace, which was probably in the garage, she speculated. She didn't recall ever seeing it, but then again, she'd never really looked. As she searched in her kitchen cabinets for a flashlight, it occurred to her that even if she found the furnace, she doubted whether she could do anything to fix the problem.

But taking some kind of action beat sitting around freezing to death.

Adam wearily replaced the receiver on his bedside phone and wiped a hand across his face. Middle-of-the-night calls from his emergency answering service were one of the down sides of his job, and he'd never quite gotten used to being jarred awake so rudely. The resulting adrenaline rush always left him restless and unable to get back to sleep.

He rose and headed to the kitchen to get a drink of water before returning the patient's call. As he reached for a glass, he glanced out the window toward the garage…and his hand froze in midair. Why were the lights on in Clare's apartment?

A sudden wave of panic engulfed him, sending another surge of adrenaline through his veins. Then he forced himself to take a deep breath. Maybe she was doing the same thing he was doing—getting a drink of water, he rationalized. Just because she was up in the middle of the night didn't mean there was a problem.

But after he drank his water and jotted a few notes about his conversation with the exchange, the light was still on. For a moment he hesitated. If all was well, Clare might consider his middle-of-the-night visit an intrusion. On the other hand, he knew he wouldn't get another wink of sleep until he assured himself that everything was okay. He'd just have to risk her annoyance, he concluded, heading for his room to pull on a pair of jeans and a sweatshirt.

Adam shivered as he stepped outside, noting that the

temperature had dropped substantially during the night. He wasted no time covering the ground between the house and garage, and when he reached the top of the stairs he rapped softly on the door.

A moment later he heard Clare's cautious voice on the other side. "Yes?"

"Clare, it's Adam. I saw your lights on. Is everything okay?"

Instead of a verbal response, he heard the lock sliding back. A moment later the door swung open.

Clare stood silhouetted by the light behind her. At least he thought it was Clare. But the apparition before him actually looked more like a mummy.

"Clare?"

She stepped aside, and now the light fell on her face. She was wrapped in some sort of quilt or comforter. "Boy, am I g-glad to s-see you!"

Her voice was shaky, and he moved beside her. "What's wrong?"

"N-no heat."

Adam suddenly became aware of the bone-chilling cold in the room. "What happened?"

"I wish I kn-knew. I just woke up a f-few minutes ago."

Now he could see the clouds of breath when she spoke. "Why didn't you call me?"

"I didn't want to bother you at this hour. Why are you up, anyway?"

"Patient call. Look, you can't stay here. Grab your coat and come back to the house. We'll deal with this tomorrow."

Instead of responding, she quickly dropped the comforter and pulled her coat out of the tiny hall closet. He held it while she slipped her arms into the sleeves, but her fingers fumbled on the buttons. Finally she gave up and just bunched it closed with one hand.

Adam preceded her out the door. "Be careful on the steps," he cautioned, eyeing her long robe. "In fact, let me go first."

She followed closely on his heels, and when they reached the bottom, he flipped off the light in the stairwell and opened the door. A blast of cold air whipped past them as they stepped outside, and Clare faltered. Instinctively, Adam reached for her hand, enfolding her delicate fingers in his. The iciness of her skin startled him, and without even stopping to consider his actions, he drew her closer to his body and placed a hand protectively around her shoulders as he guided her toward the house.

When they reached the kitchen, Adam didn't even pause. He continued toward the living room, eased her out of her coat, and gently pressed her into the chair closest to the fireplace. He retrieved the throw that was draped over the couch and tucked it around her, then knelt and set a match to the kindling in the grate. As flames began to lick up the sides of the dry wood, he returned to Clare's side. She was still shivering noticeably, and he could hear her teeth chattering. He reached for her cold hands, cocooning them in his warm clasp.

"I'll make you a cup of tea."

"Th-thank you."

When Adam returned a few minutes later and silently handed Clare a steaming mug, she sent him a grateful look. "Thank you. This looks wonderful."

But no more wonderful than she did, he realized. The flickering firelight cast a warm glow on her face, and her eyes looked large and luminous. Yet it was her hair that caught his attention. He had never seen it so loose and free before. It tumbled around her shoulders in disarray, gossamer strands of gold as fine as newly spun silk. Another rush of adrenaline that had nothing to do with his late-night patient call surged through him, and he felt an almost overpowering urge to reach out and run his fingers through her soft tresses. He stifled the impulse by jamming his fists into his pockets. What was wrong with him tonight?

Clare took several long sips of tea, then sighed contentedly and snuggled more deeply into the chair. "I'm finally starting to feel my fingers again. Thank you for coming to my rescue."

"You should have called me right away."

"I hated to bother you in the middle of the night."

"I would have been more bothered if I'd discovered that you tried to stick it out till morning. And maybe ended up with pneumonia in the process."

"I never get sick. I told you, I'm stronger than I look."

"Well, don't push your luck. I need to return a call to my patient. Will you be okay here for a few minutes?"

"Of course. Take your time."

Adam was gone longer than he expected, and by the time he returned Clare had set the empty mug beside her chair and fallen asleep. With her hair spilling over one cheek, and her face in repose, she looked younger than ever. And more fragile, somehow, despite her claim about being strong.

Adam felt a bit indiscreet, standing there watching her sleep, but he couldn't help himself. She was so lovely. And her loveliness went deeper than mere physical beauty. She was kind and sensitive and caring, and generous to a fault—much like Jo had been, he reflected. Despite her own pain, she had opened her heart to him and Nicole and given far more of herself than her job as nanny required. And because of that, she was making a huge difference in their lives.

Without conscious decision, Adam moved slowly toward her and tentatively touched her hair. It was whisper soft. Silky. And so appealing. Just like the woman.

Suddenly Adam was overcome by a longing so deep and intense that it took his breath away. Not just a longing for physical intimacy, but for an even deeper, more lasting connection. A connection of the heart, mind and soul. The kind that Jack and Theresa shared.

Jack had told him at Christmas that there was no secret to what he'd found with Theresa. It just required a willingness to reveal to special people what was in your heart. And Adam wanted to do that. Desperately. But the memories of his father's ridicule the few times he'd tried, as a youth, to express his feelings were difficult to overcome. How did you move past that? How did you learn to trust the most fragile of all your possessions—your heart—with another person?

Adam stared at Clare and drew a long, unsteady breath. He didn't know the answer to those questions. Nor was he sure he could find them. But unless he did, he would never make much headway with Nicole. She was his first priority. He needed to focus on their relationship, to find a way to welcome her into his heart. To open himself up and share.

Then maybe, if he succeeded with her, he would succeed with other relationships.

That was a big maybe, of course. And even if he got that far, even if he decided to explore another kind of relationship, he needed to move very slowly. He'd made impulsive decisions once, with Elaine, and the results had been disastrous. He wouldn't make that mistake again.

Adam raked his fingers through his hair. The whole notion of emotional intimacy was uncharted territory for him. And he couldn't exactly go out and buy a road map to show him the way. So he bowed his head and sought direction from a higher power.

Dear Lord, I know I've made a mess of things up till now in my relationships. But with Your help, I'd like to try and escape from the self-imposed emotional exile I've lived in for so long. You've already sent us a great blessing in Clare, and I thank You for that. I thank You, also, for the example of a good marriage that You've given me in Jack and Theresa. And for the insights of my brother, and his support. Please help me to listen with my heart to the guidance You are providing, and to recognize the opportunities to grow that You send my way.

I also ask that you let Clare feel Your healing presence in a special way. I know that You have given her a great cross to bear, and sometimes I think that her slender shoulders may not be able to hold it up. I see the pain and sadness in her eyes. She has been so good for us...please be good to her. Help her to find a way to replace her sorrow with joy.

And finally, Lord, please pass a message on to Jo for me. Tell her I said thank you.

"So how's the birthday girl?"

Clare smiled. "Hi, A.J. The birthday girl is trying to ignore the increasing number of candles on her cake."

"You're only as old as you feel."

"That's easy for you to say. You're the youngest."

"You aren't that far ahead of me. Did you hear from Morgan?"

"Yes. She called before she left for work. Woke me up at some uncivilized hour this morning. Apparently there's some crisis at the agency. Sometimes I think she should just close up her apartment and move into her office. She's never home, anyway."

"Tell me about it. Someone needs to give that girl a good talking-to."

"Someone did. Grant Kincaid, to be exact."

"The guy who inherited half of Aunt Jo's cottage?"

"None other. She tried to get him to meet with her on Christmas Eve to discuss it, and he told her to forget it. That it was a holiday and he was spending the time with his family."

"Good for him! I take it Morgan wasn't too happy about that?"

"Apparently not. It was still on her mind when she called today. And Christmas was two weeks ago."

"Hmm. Maybe she's finally met someone who can talk some sense into her. We can hope, anyway. But I called to talk about you. Any special plans for the day?"

"No. Just the usual."

There was a moment of silence. "You haven't told anyone it's your birthday, have you?" A.J. said, her tone slightly accusing.

"No. I don't want people to make a fuss."

An audible sigh came over the line. "I wish I was there. We'd go out on the town, have a great dinner, see a movie. Look. Promise me you'll do something special today. I don't care what it is. Just something."

"Such as?"

"I don't know. But it's important to mark the special days in our lives. Even if it's only for ourselves. Just do something out of your normal routine, okay?"

Clare smiled. "I'll do my best."

As she hung up the phone a few minutes later, Clare thought about A.J.'s request. Her sister was right, of course. And up until two years ago she'd enthusiastically embraced that same philosophy, making it a point to celebrate special days in ways that created happy memories that could be pulled out and relived on not-so-special days. But she'd gotten out of the habit since Dennis and David died. No day seemed special to her anymore. Which was a sign of depression. She'd learned that from the reading she'd done over the past two years as she'd searched in vain for solace and comfort.

But she'd promised A.J. she'd make an effort. Considering that it was an unseasonably warm day, maybe she could take a hike along Hope Creek. She'd seen the trail marker outside of town and she'd been meaning to explore. And a change of scene might help lift her spirits, which always took a nosedive on special days. Especially since she now spent most of them alone.

Clare paused and listened. The path had veered momentarily away from the creek, but she was sure she heard the splash of a waterfall through the trees. She struck off toward the sound, brushing aside the branches that blocked her way.

A couple of minutes later, she paused in delight as she emerged into a secluded, magical clearing. A small waterfall cascaded into a clear pool, and large, flat rocks were strewn along the edges. It was the kind of place where a fanciful sort of person would expect to find a leprechaun sitting on a boulder, hammering on his shoe.

A smile tipped up the corners of her mouth. That was more like something A.J. would dream up, she thought af fectionately. Her youngest sister had always had a whimsical streak. Morgan, on the other hand, had always been all business. She'd been the one who ran the lemonade stand when they were kids and devised ways to increase sales, while A.J. drank away most of the profits. Clare had been the practical one, making sure there were enough cups and napkins for the customers Morgan hoped to entice.

But right at this moment, in this place, she didn't feel practical. She felt young. And at peace. It had to be the setting, she concluded. The mist-clad mountains rose in the distance, but the sky above was cloudless, and the wind whispered in the fir trees. She lifted her face and closed her eyes, letting the sun seep into her pores. It felt so warm, so relaxing, so...

"Clare?"

Her eyelids flew open and she gasped, jerking toward the voice. At the sight of Reverend Nichols sitting on a rock a short distance away, a book in his hand, Clare's shoulders sagged in relief.

"I'm sorry. I didn't mean to startle you," he apologized. "I was engrossed in my reading, and when I looked up there you were. At least I thought it was you."

"That's okay. I didn't see you, either," Clare reassured him as she closed the distance between them. "Then again, I wasn't looking. I didn't think anyone would be here."

"I stumbled across this spot a few months ago, and I've sort of adopted it as my private hideaway. It's a great place for contemplation."

"Then I'm sorry I disturbed you."

"Not at all. I was just getting ready to go back. What brings you out on this beautiful day?"

"I've been meaning to explore the creek. And when my sister called this morning to wish me a happy birthday, she suggested I do something different to celebrate the day. So I took her advice."

"Well, you couldn't have picked a better way than to spend time in God's glorious creation. Especially on a day like this. And I think I have a perfect verse for both the place and the occasion." He flipped through his book, which Clare now realized was a pocket Bible, until he came to Psalms. "'I lift up my eyes toward the mountains; when shall help come to me?'" he read. "'My help is from the Lord, who made heaven and earth.'" He continued further down the page. "'The Lord will guard you from all evil; He will guard your life. The Lord will guard your coming and your going, both now and forever.'"

The minister's voice echoed in the stillness, and for a moment after he finished he was silent. Then he closed the book and looked up at Clare. "What better birthday present could we ask?" he said quietly.

She blinked rapidly a few times, then gave him a melancholy smile. "That's one of my sister's favorite verses."

"But not one of yours?"

The question was gentle and held no reproach. Clare studied the young minister, debating how best to answer. "I'm not sure I've experienced that verse in my life," she said slowly.

"And your sister has?"

Clare thought about his question. A.J. had suffered plenty of trauma and tragedy in her thirty-two years. Enough to last a lifetime. The loss of her fiancé. A disabling injury. Shattered dreams. Yet her faith had never wavered, as Clare's had. She still found comfort in the Bible. Even in the verse Reverend Nichols had just read.

Slowly Clare sat down on the rock across from the minister, her face troubled.

"I think so. But I'm not sure why." She recounted A.J.'s story, then shook her head. "Despite everything she went through, she never lost her connection to God, even though it didn't seem He'd been very diligent in guarding her." She sighed. "I wish I had her faith. When things got rough for me, I felt as if the Lord had abandoned me."

"Do you still feel that way?"

Clare stared at the clear stream, tumbling over the rocks a few feet away. "Most of the time. But I don't want to feel that way. It leaves an empty place deep inside that I don't know how to fill."

"I see you at church every week. Does it help?"

"More so since you became pastor. Your sermons are always wonderful. But a lot of the time I feel like I'm just going through the motions. I'm still missing the connection to the Lord that I used to have."

"Do you pray? On your own?"

"I try sometimes. But my prayers are pretty unfocused. I don't even know what to ask for, exactly."

"You mentioned that you'd had some rough times. Do you want to tell me about them?"

Clare looked over at the minister. She rarely talked about her trauma. A.J. and Morgan knew what had happened, of course. But even they didn't know about the burden of guilt she carried. She hadn't shared that with anyone. It was too painful. Too incriminating. Yet maybe she needed to talk about it, to acknowledge it, before she could let it go.

"I lost my husband and son in a car accident two years ago," she said softly.

Reverend Nichols's eyes filled with sympathy. "I'm so

sorry, Clare. I knew you were a widow, but I didn't know any of the details. One tragic death is difficult enough to deal with. Two would break a lot of people. It takes great strength to endure that kind of cross. But you survived."

She didn't respond immediately, and when she spoke her voice was a mere whisper. "Sometimes I wish I hadn't."

"A devastating loss can make a person feel that way," he said gently.

"It's not just that." She hesitated. Her heart hammered painfully in her chest, and she brushed back a stray strand of hair with an unsteady hand. "It was my fault that they died."

There was a moment of silence, and then the minister spoke again. "Are you sure about that, Clare?"

She nodded miserably. "I was at a pool party…a birth-day party…for a good friend. Dennis, my husband, had just gotten back from an overseas trip. I knew he had jet lag. But I didn't want to leave the party, so I—I asked him to drive our son to baseball practice, even though I was supposed to do it. We'd had a brief rain shower, and the pavement was slick. The accident report said h-he'd lost control of the car going around a curve on the wet road." She drew a ragged breath and buried her face in her hands. "How I wish I could believe that! But I know how tired he was. I'm so afraid that he fell asleep at the wheel. Or that he simply couldn't react quickly enough because his re-flexes were dull from fatigue. They both died as a result of my selfishness. If only I'd honored my commitment to drive David to practice, left the party when I was supposed to, I'd still have my husband and son." Her voice broke on the last word.

For a moment only the sound of the tumbling brook

could be heard in the stillness. Then Clare felt a comforting hand on her shoulder. She was almost afraid to look at Reverend Nichols, sure she would see reproach in his eyes. But when she finally did risk a glance, his eyes remained kind and nonjudgmental.

"You've made a lot of assumptions, Clare," he said gently.

"I was there, Reverend," she said, her eyes dull with pain. "I knew Dennis was tired. I should never have asked him to drive."

"Maybe not. But you don't know what really happened on that road. Maybe your husband was fully awake. Maybe an animal darted in front of the car and he tried to avoid it. Maybe when the car started to slide, there was no way to stop it no matter who was driving. Maybe if you'd been in the driver's seat, you would have been killed. Perhaps the Lord had other plans for you. Things He wanted you still to do here."

Her shoulders slumped and she looked away again. "Maybe," she said dispiritedly. "But I still feel that my selfishness was the cause of everything."

"May I tell you something, Clare? Our friendship is still new. But *selfish* is not a word I would ever use to describe you. I've seen your dedication to the Feed the Hungry program. You're at church every week, rain or shine, working in the kitchen. And I've seen what you've done for Adam and Nicole. You've put your heart and soul into the nanny job. And now that I know your story, I can only imagine how difficult that's been for you. But you're making a tremendous difference in the lives of two very lonely people who were desperately in need of help. Selfish? I don't think so. And I don't think the Lord does, either."

"I wish I could be sure of that in my heart," Clare said wistfully.

"May I make a suggestion? You said earlier that you'd tried to pray, but that you didn't know what to ask for. So don't ask for anything. Just talk to the Lord. Tell Him what's in your heart. Tell Him about your fears and your guilt and your pain. And trust that He'll give you what you need, whatever that is…release…healing…forgiveness… purpose. He'll know."

Clare looked at the minister thoughtfully. "You make it sound so simple."

"It is simple. But that doesn't mean it's easy. It can be very difficult to acknowledge that we don't have all the answers and to be open to God's guidance. In fact, we often tend to fight His direction, because it's not the path we thought we were supposed to follow. So we have to learn to listen for His voice speaking softly in our hearts, just as Elijah did in the cave. And we can't force God to respond. He always answers…but in His own time, not ours."

For the first time in two years, Clare felt hope stirring in her heart. Reverend Nichols's words had eased her burden of guilt, and he'd given her some sound advice about how to reestablish her relationship with the Lord.

It wasn't a present Clare had expected to receive on her birthday. But she couldn't think of anything she would have rather received.

Chapter Eight

"So why didn't you tell us your birthday was last week?"

Clare shot Adam a startled look across the table. "How did you know?"

"I ran into Reverend Nichols in town today. He said you two crossed paths by the creek on your birthday."

"Your birthday was last week?" Nicole stared at her. "We didn't even have a cake!"

Clare flushed. "I don't need a cake. And I stopped counting birthdays a long time ago."

"But birthdays are a big deal! We should have had a party or something!"

"I agree," Adam said. Then he turned to Clare. "Do you have anything planned tomorrow?"

She stared at him, taken aback. Her Saturdays were generally her own, except when Adam had patients in the hospital. Then she watched Nicole for a couple of hours in the morning, as she was planning to do tomorrow. "I'll be over here in the morning while you're gone. That's about it."

"Good. Then how about we go out to lunch when I get home, and afterward take the sled to Logan's Hill? I heard we're supposed to get several inches of snow tonight, now that our brief reprieve from winter is over."

Nicole and Clare stared at him incredulously, and Adam felt hot color steal up his neck. He knew his suggestion was out of character. He hadn't exactly been Mr. Spontaneous when it came to planning family outings. But for some reason, the sledding idea had popped into his mind and he'd just run with it. Though based on their looks, maybe he should have run in the other direction, he thought ruefully.

Nicole spoke first. "What sled?"

"The one I bought on the way home tonight."

"Cool!"

At least he had Nicole's approval, he thought with relief. But he wasn't so sure about Clare. When he looked at her, he saw uncertainty in the depths of her eyes. Had his suggestion triggered some unhappy memories, he wondered suddenly? It hadn't occurred to him that sledding might make her think of similar outings with her own family. The last thing he wanted to do was cause her more pain. Maybe this hadn't been such a good idea after all.

"If you'd rather do something else, just say the word," he told her. "We could go to a movie instead."

"I like the sledding idea," Nicole declared.

"But it's Clare's birthday, Nicole. So we need to pick something she'll enjoy."

Clare looked from father to daughter. She was deeply touched by Adam's gesture to recognize her birthday, although sledding wouldn't have been her first choice. It reminded her of the childhood accident that had damaged her tooth. And of similar outings with David and Dennis.

But if her goal was to help Adam and Nicole become a family, she should be encouraging them to do things like this together, not putting a damper on them. Surely she could put her own memories aside for the day.

"Sledding sounds great!" she assured him enthusiastically, hoping they wouldn't notice that the brightness in her voice was slightly forced. "But you really don't have to do anything."

"Can we get a cake, too, Dad?"

"Of course. What kind would you like, Clare?"

"Really, Adam, it's not necessary."

"She likes chocolate," Nicole told him.

"Chocolate it is, then. I'll call the bakery in the morning."

Clare capitulated with a smile. "Okay, I can see I'm being overruled here. But you have to promise me one thing. No presents."

"It's not a birthday without presents," Nicole protested.

"No presents, or I'm not going sledding," Clare said firmly.

"That's not fair," Nicole sulked.

"Hey, we did pretty good so far. Let's not push our luck," Adam told Nicole. Then he turned to Clare. "Okay. Cross my heart. No presents. Deal?"

Clare smiled at his teasing tone. "Deal."

As the dinner progressed, punctuated by easygoing conversation and laughter, Clare had the oddest feeling. It wasn't altogether unfamiliar, but it had been absent for so long that she almost didn't recognize it. Contentment.

It didn't take her long to pinpoint the reasons for her feeling of warmth and well-being. The chip on Nicole's shoulder was slowly disappearing. The relationship between father and daughter was showing definite signs of thawing. Her pain and guilt had eased slightly since she'd begun to talk to God, as Reverend Nichols had suggested. And now she had an impromptu party to look forward to with two very special people.

So much for a quiet and inconsequential birthday, she thought with a smile.

A.J. would be pleased.

"Okay, it's Clare's turn again," Nicole said, handing over the sled.

"Just one more run, then we need to leave," Clare responded. "The sun's going down. Besides, you're starting to look like Rudolph."

Nicole giggled and rubbed her nose. "I don't care. This is fun."

"Well, we've outlasted everybody, that's for sure," Adam said, surveying the deserted hill.

Clare lay on the sled, and Adam moved behind her. "Ready?" At her nod, he leaned down and grasped the edges of the runners. A moment later he gave her a hearty push.

The cold air whipped past her face as she flew down the hill, and Clare smiled both at the invigorating ride and the success of the day's outing. They'd shared a late lunch, and Nicole had been more animated than usual in anticipation of the sledding to come. She'd even teased Adam once, which had clearly delighted him. Since arriving at Logan's Hill, it had been nonstop action. And just plain fun. An unexpectedly happy, laughter-filled interlude she suspected they'd all needed desperately.

As a sudden spray of snow crystals stung her face, Clare closed her eyes for a brief moment. She didn't even see the hard clump of ice that loomed ahead and brought the sled to an abrupt stop. All she knew was that she was suddenly flying through the air, minus the sled. She opened her eyes in alarm, then quickly shut them again as she landed in a heap with a bone-jarring thud that completely knocked the breath out of her.

For several long seconds she lay unmoving, trying to coax her lungs into working again. Just when she was about to panic, they kicked into gear, and she gasped greedily, inhaling the bracing cold air.

As she concentrated on breathing in and out, she felt the hair being brushed back from her face.

"Clare? Are you all right? Don't move!"

At the undisguised panic in Adam's voice, she struggled to turn over. But a firm hand on her shoulder restrained her. "Don't move!" he repeated, his voice strained and tense.

"Dad, is she okay?" Nicole sounded scared and close to tears.

Clare took another deep breath before she tried to speak. "I'm fine," she reassured them, her voice muffled. "Adam, please let me up. I just had the wind knocked out of me."

For a moment his hand remained in place, then gradually the pressure eased. "Okay, but let's take this slow and easy."

When he rolled her onto her back, Clare almost lost her breath again. There was still panic in Adam's eyes, though it was tempered slightly now. But she saw something else, as well. Something that made her heart stir to life. Adam's worry about her condition wasn't just driven by professional concern or even friendship. He cared about her. Deeply. Not just as a person who had come to be important in his life and the life of his daughter. But as a woman.

Oddly enough, Clare wasn't even sure he recognized the depth of his feelings. Or wanted to recognize them. Which was probably good. Because she certainly wasn't ready to deal with them. Or with her own.

"Does anything hurt?"

She blinked, trying to refocus her thoughts so she could answer Adam's question. "No."

"Did you hit your head or black out, even for a second or two?"

"I don't think so."

"Okay. Let's try a couple of things."

She flexed the limbs he requested, then waited while he examined her scalp with gentle fingers.

"Everything seems to be okay," he finally said with evident relief.

She sat up. "I told you that at the beginning."

"Well, it doesn't hurt to be cautious. Come on, I'll give you a hand up and we'll get Rudolph here out of the cold."

Clare glanced at Nicole. The girl was hovering a few feet away, her red nose bright against her suddenly pale face. Obviously Adam had noticed how upset she was and was attempting to lighten the mood.

Clare put her hand in Adam's, and he pulled her to her feet in one swift, smooth motion. She was grateful for the support of his arm around her waist, however, because her legs suddenly felt very rubbery.

When she looked up, he studied her face assessingly. "Okay?"

"A little shaky. I'll be fine in a minute."

Nicole edged closer, and Clare reached out a hand. "Hey! Cheer up. You should be glad it was me that wiped out and not you. Now you guys can tease me about my rusty sledding skills."

Nicole took her hand. "Are you really okay?" she asked tremulously.

"Fine. Ask the doctor," Clare said with a smile.

"I expect she'll have a few bruises. But other than that, no harm done," he assured his daughter.

"Can we go home, then? I'm getting pretty cold now."

"Sounds like a plan to me," Clare agreed.

As they started for the car, Adam kept his arm around her waist and Nicole held tightly to her hand. Almost like a family.

Unfortunately, just not her family, she thought with a sudden, wistful pang.

Adam caught a movement out of the corner of his eye and looked up from the medical journal he was reading. Nicole was hovering in the doorway of his office, her face uncertain.

"Everything okay?" he asked.

"Yeah. I just finished my homework."

Adam waited while Nicole shifted her weight from one foot to the other.

"So…are you busy?" she finally said.

Adam closed the journal. "Not really. I can read this anytime."

She hesitated, then moved slowly into the room, her hands in her pockets. "I just wanted to make sure you really thought Clare was okay."

"She's fine. Just a little headache. She hit the ground pretty hard."

"Yeah. I was kind of scared for a minute."

"Me, too."

"Really?"

"Yeah."

Nicole perched on the edge of a chair, tension quivering in her body, like a child about to make her first jump off the high-diving board. When she spoke, her voice was quiet and a little shaky. "It made me remember how fast Mom died. I mean, one day she was taking me shopping, and the next she was gone. Like, with...with no warning."

Her voice broke, and Adam's heart contracted. He set aside the journal and leaned forward. "I'm sorry you had to go through that, Nicole. It's very hard to lose someone you love, especially when you're so young."

"I felt really alone after that. I mean, I know you took me in, but it kind of wrecked up your life. Like all of a sudden you were stuck with a kid living with you. At first I...I felt like you didn't want me. Like I was in the way. Sometimes I...I still do."

Adam felt like someone had kicked him in the gut. Instinctively he stood and moved out from behind his desk to sit on the arm of the chair beside Nicole. Tentatively he put his arm around her thin shoulders. She stiffened, but didn't pull away.

"You weren't in the way. And I did want you," he told her emphatically. "Even before the accident, I wanted to be more involved in your life, but I didn't know how. You and your mom had a special bond, and I never felt like I fit in very well. I know a lot of that's my fault. I've never been very good at expressing my feelings. But I'm learning. Because I love you, Nicole. I always have. And I'm doing my best to make us a family. I want that more than anything."

She sniffled and looked up at him. "Really?"

"Really."

She looked down again and fiddled with the hem of her sweater. "Sometimes I get scared that maybe...maybe you'll go away, too," she said in a small voice.

He swallowed hard and squeezed her shoulder. "Not if I can help it."

"But stuff…happens, you know? Like today, with Clare. I mean, she's okay and all, but what if she wasn't?"

That thought had occurred to Adam, as well. And it left him with a sick feeling in the pit of his stomach. So he couldn't very well try to placate Nicole. "Then we'd have to do the best we could. We'd have to take care of each other. We'll have to do that anyway, when she leaves at the end of May."

"I know. But that's months away. And we can still be friends with her even after she leaves, can't we?"

"Of course."

Nicole frowned. "But it won't be the same. I'll miss her a lot."

Adam didn't know how to respond to that. Because he was beginning to feel exactly the same way.

Things were not looking good. Clare added the columns of figures once more—with the same discouraging results.

With a sigh, she reached for her mug of tea and took a fortifying sip. Although she was doing her best to stretch her limited resources over the six months of her nanny job, she'd already blown her budget. Living rent free helped immensely, but the root canal and some major repair work on her car had put a huge dent in her bank account. If everything went smoothly for the next three and a half months, she might be able to eke it out. But she couldn't count on that. Another emergency could easily arise.

And if it did, where could she turn for help? She couldn't ask A.J. Her youngest sister had lived on subsistence wages for years. And Morgan was having her own financial problems. So she needed to build up her cash reserves in case of another emergency.

Which left her only one option.

"I saw Clare at Wal-Mart yesterday."

Adam continued writing in Adele's chart. "Is that right?" he replied distractedly.

"She works too hard, Adam. You should talk to her. Between taking care of Nicole and cooking your meals, not to mention helping out at church and at Nicole's school on a regular basis, I'm sure she has her hands full. She doesn't need another job."

Adam stopped writing and looked up at Adele. "What did you say?"

"I said I think you should talk to her about taking on this second job."

Adam had only half listened to Adele's chitchat, but now he tried to focus on what she'd said. She'd mentioned running into Clare at…Wal-Mart. And what was this about a second job?

"I'm sorry, Adele. Did you say Clare had a second job?"

She raised her eyebrows. "You didn't know?"

"No."

"Hmm. Clare's working at Wal-Mart."

Adam frowned. "How long has that been going on?"

"Just a couple of weeks, from what I could gather. I asked why she didn't just substitute teach, but apparently she'd have to get different credentials in North Carolina."

Adam's frown deepened. Since early February, things had gone crazy at the office as a flu epidemic swept the county. He'd been getting home far later than usual, too exhausted to do anything but wolf down his dinner and head for bed. He and Clare had hardly exchanged more than a few words all month. So he had no idea what had prompted her need for a second job. But he intended to find out tonight.

"Thanks for letting me know, Adele. I'll definitely look into it."

"Good. I hate to see her wearing herself down."

Adam jotted down a prescription, then tore it off and handed it to Adele. "This should help those sinuses."

She tucked it into her purse and rose. "You're a good doctor, Adam. I'm sure this will solve my problem. Now take care of your nanny."

"Clare, could I talk with you for a minute?"

At the serious tone in Adam's voice, Clare turned from the sink. "Is everything all right?"

"That's what I'd like to find out. Is Nicole doing her homework?"

"Yes."

"Let's sit for a minute, okay?"

Clare wiped her hands on the dish towel and carefully draped it over the sink. Something in Adam's tone put her on alert, and when she joined him at the kitchen table a moment later she gingerly eased into a chair and folded her hands nervously in front of her.

For a moment he didn't speak, and she studied his face. He looked bone weary, she thought. Which wasn't surprising, since he'd put in a ridiculous number of hours over the past month. While the workload was finally beginning to abate, the pressures and demands had left their mark. The fine lines that radiated from the corners of his eyes had deepened, and the smudges beneath them spoke of late hours and interrupted sleep. The fingers he'd wrapped around his coffee cup seemed slightly unsteady, as well.

"I saw Adele today," he said at last.

"Is she okay?"

"Yes. But she passed on some disturbing information. She told me that you had taken a part-time job."

Clare frowned, momentarily caught off guard. "Yes. But I only work nine to two, four days a week. We agreed that my time was my own while Nicole was in school."

"It is. But I didn't expect you to go out and get another job."

She sent him a curious look. She hadn't purposely kept the part-time job a secret. But with Adam's hectic schedule, there'd been no real opportunity to bring it up. She wasn't sure why it was such a big deal. Unless he felt awkward about having his nanny work at Wal-Mart.

"I would have done substitute teaching if I had the right credentials for North Carolina," she said. "But since I didn't, this was the most convenient thing I could find. I didn't mean to embarrass you."

Now it was his turn to frown. "This isn't about me, Clare. You could never do anything to embarrass me. I'm more concerned about why you felt the need to take on another job. It seems to me we keep you plenty busy here at the house, and I know you help out at church and at Nicole's school. I don't mean to pry into your personal business, but have you had some sort of financial emergency? Because if that's the case, I'd certainly be happy to help."

Although she was touched by Adam's generosity, accepting such an offer wouldn't be in keeping with the spirit of Aunt Jo's will. Besides, it was important to her to be self-reliant. She drew a deep breath, then looked directly into his eyes. "I appreciate that, Adam. But there's no immediate emergency. I just want to build up a little reserve. The root canal and car repairs pretty much wiped me out."

Adam took a moment to digest that. When they'd first met, Clare had implied that she'd fallen on tough financial times. But apparently they were even tougher than he'd imagined. Which explained why she was so in need of Jo's legacy. And why she'd taken on a second, low-paying job. Yet at one time she'd obviously enjoyed a far different lifestyle. What had happened to reduce her to such a desperate state? It wasn't any of his business, of course. And she hadn't offered details. But he wanted to know.

"You can tell me to mind my own business if you want to, and I won't be offended," he said slowly. "But what happened, Clare? You obviously weren't always in such dire straits."

As she searched his kind, caring eyes, Clare was torn between the need to share her burden and the need to protect Dennis's memory. She didn't want anyone to think badly of her husband because he had left her with so little in a material sense. That's why she'd never revealed her precarious financial situation, even to her sisters. Dennis had loved his family with an intensity that had sometimes taken her breath away. He had done everything he could to provide them with the best of everything. And he'd planned to continue doing so.

He just hadn't planned on dying.

Clare blinked rapidly, then reached up to brush back a few stray strands of hair that had worked their way loose from her chignon. For more than two long years she'd carried her burden alone, struggling to make ends meet even as she dealt with her grief. There had been times when she'd been utterly discouraged, had longed for a sympathetic shoulder to cry on. Figuratively speaking, anyway, because Clare didn't cry. She hadn't shed one tear since the accident. At first she'd been too shocked even to react. Shock had been followed by numbness, which in turn had given way to an emptiness that had left her heart devoid of everything—even tears. Which wasn't the best way to deal with grief. She knew that. Tears were therapeutic. But she was afraid that if she gave in to her grief she'd sink into a pit of despair from which she would never emerge.

So she'd held her tears inside and somehow managed to find the strength to carry on alone. But she was tired of being alone. Lately she'd felt an almost desperate longing to share her burden with someone. To share what it had been like to wake up one morning and realize that her whole world had changed forever in the blink of an eye. And as she gazed into Adam's kind, warm eyes, she suddenly knew that he was the one she wanted to share it with.

"It's kind of a long story," she said.

"I have all evening."

"You may be sorry." Clare tried to smile, but couldn't quite pull it off.

"I don't think so."

"Well, I'll try to give you the condensed version." She paused for a moment to collect her thoughts, then took a deep breath. "When I was twenty-five, I met a wonderful man named Dennis. He was kind and smart and outgoing, and I fell head over heels in love. We were married a year later. And two years after that we…we had a son."

"David." At her startled look, Adam explained. "Nicole told me about him."

She nodded. "We were so happy! I gave up teaching to be a full-time mom, and Dennis's star started to rise. Within a few years he had an executive position in public relations with a major agency. I was happy for him because he'd come from a dirt-poor family where no one had ever gotten a college education, and success meant a lot to him. So did the trappings of success. We had a beautiful home in an exclusive suburb of Kansas City, and we sent David to one of the finest schools in the area. We took fabulous vacations, and Dennis lavished us with gifts. We had the best of everything, from clothes to cars to home furnishings."

Clare paused, and when she spoke again her voice had dropped. "The thing is, Dennis didn't expect to die. He was young and healthy and had many more years to work. To save. To pay off all our debts. At least that's what we thought. But the accident changed everything. In every way. They were both…" She paused and sucked in a sharp breath. "They both died," she said in a choked voice.

Adam looked down at her tightly clasped hands. He ached to reach over and cover them with his own, to comfort her for the loss of her family and her dreams. But he remained still, knowing she had more to say.

"Afterwards, I realized just how deeply in debt we were," she continued unsteadily. "We had a huge mortgage on the house, and we'd heavily financed the cars…as well as other things. Dennis had some life insurance, but it wasn't anywhere near enough to cover our financial obligations. It was clear that everything would have to go."

She raised her head and gave Adam an intent, almost fierce look. "But I didn't really care about those things, anyway. They were important to Dennis, and I understood that, given his background. I grew up on a farm, and while we never lived lavishly, we always had nice clothes and plenty to eat. So I never attached as much importance to material things. It wasn't hard for me to give them up."

It was obviously important to her that Adam understand she held nothing against her husband for not providing for her after his death. But Adam wasn't so generous. A man with a family, who chose to live so close to the edge of financial ruin, should at the very least have considered the possibility of an accident and provided for the welfare of those he loved. Adam had little sympathy for such irresponsibility. But he kept those thoughts to himself.

"So then what happened?" he prompted gently.

"I sold almost everything and moved into an apartment. I knew I'd have to go back to work, so I got recertified as a teacher. I was just starting to substitute teach on a regular basis when Aunt Jo's legacy fell in my lap. I still have some debts to pay off, and I'd like to establish a little financial reserve. So her bequest was a godsend. I'll be fine once I can claim it, but in the meantime I need to generate some income. Things are a little…tight."

He suspected that was a gross understatement. She was clearly living a bare-bones existence, purchasing only the absolute necessities. Yet she truly didn't seem to mind.

But something didn't quite make sense, he realized with a frown. "Given your situation, I'm surprised Jo didn't provide some sort of stipend for you while you worked as our nanny. Sort of an advance against the bequest. She wasn't the type to ever leave a need unaddressed."

Clare averted her face. "She didn't know about the state of my finances. No one does."

He didn't have to ask why she'd kept that information to herself. Clare was protecting Dennis's memory. Which he admired. But loyalty to her late husband wasn't going to solve her problem. Clearly she needed a temporary job, for her own peace of mind if nothing else. And teaching was out of the question. Still, there had to be something that would make better use of her skills than clerking at the giant discount store.

Suddenly, in a flash, a solution presented itself. He wasn't sure she'd go for it. But it was certainly worth a try.

"I may have an idea," he said slowly.

She looked at him curiously but remained silent.

"When Janice has her baby, she'll be taking six weeks off. The temp I had lined up just fell through, so I'm desperate for a replacement starting next Monday. I only need someone from eight to four, four days a week. Nicole's gone by seven-thirty, and she could stay at the after-school program for half an hour. You'd still have Wednesdays free to work with the Feed the Hungry program if you wanted. You'd be perfect for the job, Clare."

She stared at him. Working as a temporary receptionist in Adam's office was far preferable to stocking shelves at Wal-Mart, but was it somehow violating the spirit of Jo's legacy?

As if he'd read her mind, Adam spoke. "Jo's stipulation about pay related to the nanny job," he pointed out. "If you don't take the receptionist job, I'll still have to fill it. I'll be paying the same salary whether it's to you or to someone else. And I guarantee you'll have a great boss," he added with a grin.

Some of the tension in Clare's shoulders eased, and she smiled in return. She couldn't argue with his logic. And it was the perfect solution to her problem. "You've convinced me. I accept. But I've never done this kind of work before. I hope you won't be sorry."

"Not a chance," he assured her.

Which was true. He already knew Clare was sharp and quick. She'd have the office routine mastered in a couple of days. It was the ideal solution to her problem. And his.

Not to mention the fact that for the next six weeks, he would get to see a whole lot more of his daughter's nanny.

Chapter Nine

"Adam, may I interrupt you for a moment?"

At Clare's slightly uncertain voice, Adam paused and glanced up from the chart he was reviewing on his way to the next examining room. "What is it?"

"There's a Mrs. Samuels on the line. I know you have back-to-back patients today, but I think you might want to take this. I checked her records and saw that she's diabetic. It sounds like she may be having problems with her insulin."

The twin furrows in Adam's brow deepened. "Pull the chart and put her through to my office."

Clare handed him the chart. "She's waiting on line three."

Adam nodded. "Let Mr. Travis know I'll be right with him."

A few minutes later, as Adam hung up the phone, he was reminded again of how quickly Clare had become a valued member of his staff. After only two weeks, she had not only learned the office routine, but took appropriate initiative and demonstrated sound judgment with patients.

Like Janice, she was able to screen calls and quickly discern the true emergencies. Today she'd been right on the money in her assessment of Mrs. Samuels's condition. The woman had needed immediate attention, and Clare had recognized that.

As he strode down the hall, Adam took a moment to pause at the receptionist's counter. "Good call," he told Clare.

She gave him a relieved smile. "Thanks."

"Mary Beth, could you do a throat swab on Mrs. Reed in room four? We might have a case of strep."

"Sure thing."

The two women watched as Adam continued down the hall, then Mary Beth turned to Clare with a grin. "Congrats on the accolades. They were well deserved. I have to admit I was a little nervous about Janice being gone, but you've really picked things up quickly. It's been smooth as silk. Don't tell Janice I said that, though. She might get nervous about her job."

Clare laughed. "She doesn't need to worry. This is very definitely a temporary position for me."

"I don't know. Adam runs a tight ship, and he seems really pleased. He might not want to let you go."

Clare knew Mary Beth was just teasing, so she only smiled in response. But more and more, she was finding herself wishing that were true. And not just about the receptionist job. It was silly, of course. Adam clearly wasn't in the market for romance. Despite what she'd seen in his eyes the day of the sledding accident, he'd never done anything to suggest directly he had an interest in her beyond the jobs she was doing for him. His primary goal was to establish a close relationship with his daughter. Clare was simply a catalyst for that.

And frankly, even if he was interested in her in a more…personal way, she wasn't ready to offer him much encouragement. She was trying to work through her guilt over the accident, but it was slow going. And until she resolved that, she couldn't really mourn the loss of her beloved family. So she wasn't ready to think about the future yet, either.

But as she watched Adam interact with his patients at work and strive so diligently at home to be the kind of father he had never known, she recognized what a fine and caring person he was. His patients loved him for his empathetic and unassuming bedside manner, and Clare had been struck time and again by his warmth and patience. No matter how tired or stressed he was, no matter how many demands he was trying to juggle, when he sat down with patients they generally had his full and complete attention. He was an insightful listener who was able to quickly asses a condition and then make sound and decisive decisions. Clare now understood why the town felt so fortunate to have him. He truly was a superb doctor.

He wasn't quite as far along on the father front, but he was making great strides. Where once Clare had had to struggle to get Nicole to include Adam in the dinner conversation, the two of them now talked more easily and naturally without her intervention. And she'd noticed that, more and more, Nicole was seeking out Adam for advice. There were even occasional moments of physical affection, when Adam would put his hand on Nicole's shoulder or she would jab him playfully in the arm. While there was still a lot of room for improvement, the trend was in the right direction. And both father and daughter were blossoming because of it.

Which was good. Because with only a couple of

months remaining in her nanny commitment, she was running out of time to help those two become a family.

"A penny for your thoughts."

Startled, Clare shot Adam a guilty look, embarrassed at being caught daydreaming. "They're not for sale," she told him with a smile. "Did you need something?"

Clare saw something flicker for a brief moment in his eyes, something that made her breath catch in her throat. But then he simply handed her Mr. Travis's chart. "Could you write up an order for blood work?"

"Sure."

As he walked away, she tried to quiet the sudden staccato beat of her heart. Though the look in his eyes had been brief, she was pretty sure she had identified it correctly.

Longing.

And she felt exactly the same way.

But until she dealt with her personal issues, and until Adam recognized—and acknowledged—his own feelings, there was nothing to do but wait.

"Boy, this is a great spot! The furniture's new, isn't it? Seems to me the last time we were here this porch was bare."

Adam leaned forward to lift his mug from the wicker coffee table, then settled back into the comfortable matching chair before he replied to his brother, "You get an A for your powers of observation," he said with a wry smile. "Clare found the whole set at an estate sale, including the settee you've appropriated."

Jack chuckled. "As I recall, you hogged the couch at Christmas. Now it's my turn." He sighed contentedly. "This is the life."

"I'm glad you're enjoying our hospitality."

"The amenities have improved considerably since the last time we were here. And there's actually a bed in the guest room now. No more sleeping bags."

"Clare found that at the same estate sale."

"And the food is better, too. No more take-out from that café in town for every meal."

"Clare's a good cook."

"She seems to be good at a lot of things."

Adam nodded. "She's worked wonders with Nicole."

"I've noticed. The prickly pear has been replaced by a peach."

"Clever, but true," Adam said with a smile. "And we're getting along better than ever. My only concern is what will happen when Clare leaves. I'm afraid Nicole will be devastated."

Jack eyed his brother speculatively. "And how about her father?"

Adam stared into his coffee. "I'm trying not to think about that," he said quietly.

"Why not?"

He gave a frustrated sigh and raked his fingers through his hair. "Clare's had a lot of trauma in her life already. She doesn't need any more. And I'm just not husband material. My wife would have told you that."

"Maybe you just had the wrong wife."

"Maybe. But I had a tough time with Nicole, too. I have trouble with relationships in general. I think I'm getting better, but I wouldn't want to risk hurting Clare—even if she was open to romance. Which I don't think she is. She loved her husband very much. She still does."

"Just because she loved her husband doesn't mean there isn't room in her heart for someone else. And I've seen the way she looks at you. My guess is that her interest is more than professional."

Adam felt his heart stop, then race on. "Even if that was true, I can't risk hurting her," he said carefully. "I wouldn't want to be married again unless I could have something like you and Theresa have. But that takes a willingness to open up and to share your feelings and emotions. I'm still fighting Dad's legacy on that front."

"Let me ask you something, Adam. Do you trust Clare?"

"Of course."

Jack sat up and dismissed Adam's response with an impatient shake of his head. "I don't mean do you trust her to keep the records correctly at your office, or to tutor Nicole or to handle your household budget. I'm talking about trust at the deepest level. Do you trust that no matter what you tell her about your past, about your deepest fears and your dreams and your feelings, that she'll always treat you gently?"

Adam frowned. Leave it to Jack to ask the tough questions. Adam turned toward the distant, blue-hazed mountains and thought back over the many examples of Clare's empathy and caring that he'd witnessed: the gifts she'd lovingly knitted for him and Nicole at Christmas, her generous work with the Feed the Hungry program, her efforts to help Nicole make friends at school, the way she'd transformed his house into a home—a place he relished returning to after a long day. He thought about her keen insights and gentle kindness, honed in the fire of adversity. About her loyalty to the ones she loved, and about the way she was miraculously transforming the lives of two lonely people. Trust Clare? The answer was obvious.

"Yes."

"Then what's holding you back?"

Jack's question was not only pointed, but valid. And Adam knew the answer, though it was difficult to articulate after years of living with a father who saw such admissions as weakness. Adam glanced down into the murky depths of his coffee and forced himself to give voice to the word. "Fear."

"Bingo," Jack concurred quietly. "And you know what? That's not a sin, Adam, despite what Dad might have made you think. It's okay to be afraid. I've been afraid. A lot of times. And Theresa knows it. That didn't hurt our relationship. In fact, it made it stronger. Being willing to admit that you don't always have all the answers, that sometimes you're afraid and uncertain, is just being human. Superheroes might be nice in the movies, but in a relationship nobody wants a perfect mate. That would be impossible to live with—or live up to. People just want someone who cares, who tries to understand their point of view, their feelings, their fears, their hopes—and who's willing to share theirs. That doesn't mean you're always perfect. It just means you sincerely try." He paused for a moment and took a deep breath. "May I tell you something else?"

Adam looked up, but remained silent.

"You're just about there, buddy. I can't believe the difference in you in the past few months. You look happier and more relaxed than I've ever seen you. And you've shared more with me in our last couple of visits than you have in our entire lives. I'd say that's progress. And my guess is that one very special nanny can take the credit for that."

Jack leaned forward, clasped his hands and rested his forearms on his thighs. "So here's a piece of advice from your kid brother, for whatever it's worth. If I were you, I'd think long and hard about renewing Clare's contract— on a permanent and personal basis."

As they settled into the church pew for the sermon, Clare glanced at the family group next to her. Nicole was on her left, with Adam beside her. Theresa was next in the row, then came Adam's niece and nephew, Karen and Bobby. Jack was at the end of the pew, on the aisle.

When Adam and Nicole had insisted that she join in the family's Easter activities, she'd hesitated, not wanting to intrude. But in the end, she was glad they had talked her into it. She'd liked Jack and Theresa immediately, and they had embraced her warmly, making her feel like part of the group instead of an outsider. Under Jack's energetic direction, there had been nonstop activity since their arrival. And Clare was glad for that. It gave her less time to think about past Easters, when she'd had her own family.

Reverend Nichols moved to the pulpit, and Clare focused her attention on him. As usual, his sermon was well prepared and articulate. And his final words touched her deeply.

"A few years ago, shortly after I was ordained, I was assisting at a church in a small town in Oklahoma," he said. "I preached what I thought was a very good sermon, and I was eagerly waiting to greet the congregation afterward, sure I'd receive all kinds of accolades.

"Well, things didn't go quite as I expected. Most people said polite, perfunctory things. But no one raved. Finally an older gentleman came along. At that point I was desperate for a compliment, so I asked him if he'd enjoyed the sermon. And I'll never forget what he said to me.

"'It was okay, young man. But if you want people to really listen, you need to speak from the heart. Facts and figures are all well and good, and I expect I learned a thing or two today about Bible history. But that's not going to make me change my life. Don't just tell me what I'm supposed to believe. Tell me why *you* believe it. What's in the heart is just as important as what's in the head.'

"Well, needless to say, my ego was pretty deflated. But when I thought about it, I realized he was right. And I took his comments to heart. But I can tell you that his advice isn't always easy to follow. Because when we speak from the heart about our faith, we take a risk. We're not just putting our theology on the line, we're putting ourselves on the line. We're opening ourselves to ridicule and rejection and pain. And in the case of our Lord, to death. But the important thing to remember is that His death wasn't the end. It was the beginning.

"My dear friends, that's what Easter is all about. The lessons of this day are many, but a key one is that we must live what we believe, not just think about it. We must follow our Lord's example of complete and unselfish love. Sometimes that means we have to take chances. That in order to grow in our faith, and in our lives, we have to be willing to trust our heart with other people. To share what we believe, knowing that not everyone will treat us kindly. Knowing that we can become discouraged and afraid. But unless we let go of our fear, unless we follow the example of our Lord and reach out to other people with our love, we can never move forward or fulfill His plan for us.

"So on this Easter Sunday, as we celebrate new life in Christ, I ask Him to bestow the gift of His grace on all of us, and to give us the courage to trust in Him and to love as He did...completely, selflessly and without reservation. And now let us pray...."

Clare felt tears welling up in her eyes at the beautiful message in Reverend Nichols's sermon. Unconsciously she looked to Adam, wondering if the message had special meaning for him, as well.

But he was turned toward Jack. And as she watched, a brief, knowing look passed between the two brothers.

Feeling like an eavesdropper, Clare quickly turned back toward the front. But she couldn't help wondering what that look was all about.

"Do you think Dad will be surprised?"

Clare turned toward Nicole, who was setting the table. Fresh flowers were arranged in a glass bowl in the center of the snowy-white cloth, and there was a festive feel in the air. "Absolutely. I think he's convinced we've forgotten his birthday entirely. I didn't say a word to him about it this morning."

"Me, neither."

Clare flipped the switch for the oven light and checked the meat thermometer. "Looks like we're about ready. Now let's hope the guest of honor is on time."

As if on cue, they heard the sound of crunching gravel as Adam's car pulled up the driveway to the garage.

"Showtime," Clare said with a smile.

Nicole nervously wiped her hands on her oversize apron. "I hope he likes everything."

"Pork tenderloin, potatoes au gratin, green beans almondine—and a killer birthday cake—what's not to like?" Clare said encouragingly.

"Yeah. I guess."

A moment later they heard the door open. Adam strode into the room—but then stopped abruptly as his gaze fell on the beautifully set table, then traveled to the Happy Birthday banner and balloons that decorated the room.

"Happy birthday, Dad."

He heard the barely suppressed excitement—as well as the touch of uncertainty—in Nicole's voice, and gave her his full attention. "I thought everyone had forgotten."

She giggled. "We wanted to surprise you. That's why we didn't say anything all day."

Adam looked at Clare. "So you were in on this, too, huh?"

She smiled. "Guilty. But it was mostly your daughter's doing. In fact, she cooked most of the dinner."

"It smells wonderful."

"Well, it's all ready. Go ahead and sit down, Dad."

Adam did as instructed, and while Clare and Nicole set out the food, he couldn't help recalling last year's birthday. There had been no celebration. Nothing at all to mark the occasion. If Nicole had even remembered that the day held special significance, she had chosen to ignore it. His childhood memories weren't much better. The only concession to birthdays in his father's house had been a cake for dessert. Even during his marriage, he and Elaine had simply gone out for dinner—usually to a restaurant of her choosing. He had never had a birthday like this, in his own home, with decorations and a dinner cooked especially for him. He felt his throat grow tight, and there was an odd stinging sensation behind his eyes.

"Would you like to say grace, Adam?"

At Clare's gentle voice, he looked up, noting that she and Nicole had taken their places. Forcing himself to swallow past the lump in his throat, he nodded and bowed his head.

"We thank You, Lord, for this wonderful meal, and for the gift of special people in our lives. We thank You for the many blessings You give us, for Your comfort and companionship in times of trouble, and for the joy and peace that comes from knowing You are always with us, in good times and bad. I ask Your special blessing today on Nicole and Clare, who have given me a birthday to remember. Please watch over them and keep them in Your care. Amen."

When he finished, the wistful look in Clare's momentarily unguarded eyes told him that his words had touched her deeply.

Adam couldn't remember when he'd enjoyed a meal more. The food Nicole had prepared was wonderful—thanks, he was sure, to Clare's close supervision—but even better was the company. Nicole chatted animatedly throughout the meal, and the easy banter among the three of them was in marked contrast to the silent, strained meals he and Nicole had shared prior to Clare's arrival. He had only one word to describe the transformation that had occurred in his relationship with his daughter: *miracle.*

Which was exactly what he'd prayed for. Thanks to an unexpected nanny. Adam thought back to his early conversations with Clare, how her surprising offer hadn't been exactly the kind of help he'd had in mind when he'd asked the Lord for assistance. But he also recalled reminding himself at the time that God's ways weren't always our ways. And that maybe Clare was the answer to his prayer.

As he regarded the lovely woman sitting across from

him, he suddenly knew there were no maybes about it. Recalling Jack's advice, he also knew exactly what he was going to wish for when he blew out the candles on his cake.

"I can't eat one more bite," Adam groaned as he finished off a second slice of the split lemon torte.

"So it was okay?" Nicole asked anxiously.

He grinned. "It was more than okay. It was the best birthday cake I ever had."

She smiled, and the pleasure in her eyes warmed his heart. "Cool!"

He reached over and gave her shoulder a squeeze. "You can cook for me anytime."

"Well, I couldn't have done it without Clare. She showed me how to make all the stuff."

"Then my hat is off to Clare, too," he acknowledged.

"And did you like your presents?"

Adam smiled. Nicole had given him the latest detective novel by his favorite author, and Clare had knitted him an incredible fisherman's sweater. He couldn't even begin to guess how many hours it had taken her to complete it.

"They were wonderful." His compliment encompassed both of his dinner companions, and a becoming flush spread over Clare's cheeks.

His response obviously satisfied Nicole, too. "I guess we did okay, huh, Clare?"

She smiled. "I guess we did."

Nicole turned back to Adam. "So do you have to work tonight?"

"Not unless someone calls."

"Good. Then we can play a game before I do my homework. You're supposed to have games at parties."

Adam grinned. "I don't think I'll be very good at pin the tail on the donkey."

She gave him a what-planet-are-you-from? look. "Dad, that is prehistoric! Nobody does stuff like that anymore. I borrowed a game from Candace that we played at her slumber party. It's called Revelation."

He wasn't sure he liked the sound of that. "How does it work?"

"Well, everyone draws ten cards, and each card has a question. Like, 'What's your middle name?' or 'What are you most afraid of?' Stuff like that. And you write your answers down. Then all of the questions get put in a pile, you draw them one by one, and everyone has to guess who wrote what answer. The person who guesses right most often wins."

Adam shifted uncomfortably. The game sounded a little too personal to him. He was trying to be more open about his feelings, but he wasn't sure he was up to something this potentially revealing. Even though he could almost hear Jack telling him to loosen up, he just wasn't there yet.

Adam was literally saved by the bell when his pager went off. Trying not to look too relieved, he reached for it and read the message. "I need to call the exchange," he said when he finished.

Nicole made a face. "But it's your birthday."

"People still get sick." He stood and put his hand on her shoulder. "Why don't you start that homework, and we'll try to fit the game in later?"

She sighed. "Okay."

"Hey." He leaned down. "Even if we don't get to the game, this is still the best birthday I ever had."

She searched his eyes. "Really?"

"Really."

A smile lifted the corners of her mouth. "I'm glad."

"Now you scoot, and I'll take care of this call." He stood and looked over at Clare. "I'll be back in a few minutes."

"Take your time. I'll get the dishes started."

Adam took as long as he possibly could with the call, and by the time he returned Clare had restored the kitchen to order.

"Everything okay?" she asked.

"Yes. Is there any coffee left?"

She checked the pot. "Looks like a couple of cups. Would you like some more?"

"I'll get it." He helped himself, then glanced toward the hall.

"I mentioned to Nicole that you were probably tired after working all day and might not be up to the game," Clare told him.

He shot her a grateful look. "Thanks."

She dried her hands on a dish towel, then folded it carefully and set it on the counter. "You didn't seem too anxious to play."

He took a sip of coffee. "I'm not sure it's my kind of game."

She looked at him. "That's what I figured."

What else did she figure, he wondered. Even though he'd been careful not to reveal too much about himself, this insightful woman seemed to understand things about him that he barely understood himself. Which was more than a little disconcerting.

But also encouraging. Because she hadn't backed off at his reticence, nor had she seemed put off by any negative conclusions she'd come to. Adam had told Jack that he trusted Clare. But he hadn't actually done anything to prove that. Maybe tonight was the time to see if he could live what he said he believed, as Reverend Nichols had suggested in his Easter sermon four weeks before.

"I thought I might sit on the porch for a while. It's a beautiful night. Would you like to join me?" he asked, striving for a casual, conversational tone.

Clare looked at him in surprise. The porch, with its wicker furniture and its restful view of blue-hazed mountains across the valley, was one of her favorite spots. But Adam rarely had the time—or took the time, she corrected herself—to enjoy it. She was glad he wanted to take advantage of it tonight. It would be a nice ending to his birthday.

"Sure. Let me grab a sweater."

He waited until she reappeared from the mudroom, a light sweater slung over her shoulders, then followed her to the front porch. Clare sat on the settee, assuming Adam would choose the matching chair at right angles. But to her surprise he settled in beside her, their bodies just a whisper apart. As the faint but heady scent of his aftershave filled her nostrils, her pulse suddenly vaulted into overdrive and her breath lodged in her chest.

Clare was completely taken aback by her reaction to Adam's close proximity. And she was more than a little frightened when a surge of longing swept over her, so strong it stole the breath from her lungs. Trying not to be obvious, she discreetly attempted to put a little more distance between them. But she was already wedged against the unyielding arm of the settee. Short of getting up and calling attention to her predicament, she had no choice but to remain where she was.

"Jack really enjoyed this spot while they were here for Easter," Adam remarked, clearly oblivious to her dilemma.

Clare swallowed. It had been a long time since she'd had a reaction like this to a man. Visceral, powerful—and ill timed. She wasn't ready to get involved with any man. Especially this man, who was struggling with his own demons. Get a grip! she admonished herself, drawing in a long, steadying breath.

"I know you guys spent a lot of time out here one evening," she replied, struggling to keep her voice even. "He and Theresa are really a nice couple."

"They have something special," Adam agreed. "And I'm happy for them, of course. But sometimes…well, I guess I'm a little…envious."

She could relate to that. Watching Jack and Theresa interact over the holiday had been a bittersweet reminder of the good times she'd enjoyed with Dennis. "It's hard to be alone," Clare said quietly.

He shook his head. "It's not just that. I don't even have happy memories to fall back on, like you do. Even when we were at our best, Elaine and I…we never related the way Jack and Theresa do. We were never that much…in sync."

Clare had a feeling that they were moving on to untried ground. Though she had on occasion glimpsed deeply felt emotions in Adam's eyes, he had never before spoken of anything this personal. The closest he had come was the day of Nicole's party, when he'd alluded to his emotionally bleak childhood.

"Maybe you and your wife just weren't compatible," she ventured cautiously.

"That was certainly part of it," he conceded with a sigh. "We got way too serious way too fast. And that was my fault." He paused, and his voice was more halting when he resumed speaking, as if he had to dig deep to find the words. "I had...very few friends growing up. And I didn't date much. So I was completely blown away when Elaine took an interest in me. Later, when things started to fall apart, I realized that she...she had always been more interested in being married to a doctor than to me."

Knowing what a tight rein he kept on his feelings and emotions, and how carefully he protected his heart, Clare could only imagine what that admission had cost him.

"It sounds to me like there was fault on both sides," she said gently.

"Mostly mine. When I was growing up, my father...he made fun of us if we showed emotion—of any kind. He thought it was a sign of weakness. Jack was able to get past that and march to the beat of his own drummer. That's probably why he has such a happy marriage. But I...I wasn't as strong as he was. I cared what my father thought and tried to please him. Though I never did, of course. So I gradually closed up. And eventually I...I lost the ability to express emotions and to...connect with people."

Clare frowned. "That's not true, Adam. I've seen you with your patients. They love you. You have a wonderful bedside manner."

He dismissed her comment with a frustrated shake of his head. "That's different. It's all one-sided. They teach you how to listen and be sympathetic in medical school. But on a personal level, when you're trying to establish a relationship with the people you love, it has to be a two-way street. Listening isn't enough. You have to share with them, too. Let them see what's in your heart. I've never been able to do that."

He expelled a long sigh, and when he took a sip of his coffee Clare noticed that his hand wasn't quite steady.

"Eventually, that's what turned Elaine off. Despite the fast courtship, despite the fact we married for the wrong reasons, maybe we could have worked things out if I'd been willing to let her in. But I couldn't. Instead, I began focusing more and more on the one area of my life where I felt capable—medicine. Which only made matters worse. And over time, any love between us died quietly, gradually slipping away, until one day it was simply gone."

"But you stayed together a long time," Clare pointed out.

He gave a short, mirthless laugh. "Yeah. But not for the noblest reasons. The one thing Elaine and I had going for us was…" He paused and shifted uncomfortably. "I guess chemistry is the right word. On a physical level. If it hadn't been for that, we would have separated far sooner. So I'm a bit wary of…physical attraction. Because it's not enough to sustain a marriage over the long haul."

"I agree."

"Anyway, I'm just not good at opening up. Of letting people get close. And you can't connect with people if you don't. My relationship with Nicole is a good example."

"But that's improving. You two are getting along better all the time."

"Thanks to you."

Clare shook her head. "I might have helped set the stage, but you had to step into the role. And you've done a wonderful job. In fact, I'd call it remarkable, now that I know more about your background. Because you didn't have a lot of tools to work with."

Adam set his mug on the coffee table and turned to

Clare. How did she always know the right things to say, he wondered. "You know something, Clare? I love the sweater you knitted for me. It's a wonderful birthday gift. But what you just said is the best gift of all. I just wish I could believe it was true."

The sincerity in her eyes was unquestionable. "Trust me, Adam. It is."

There was that word again. *Trust.* He angled his body toward her and, without stopping to think, reached for her hand and brushed his thumb across her silky skin. "I prayed for help with Nicole," he said, his voice not quite steady. "And I've come to believe that God sent me you. And maybe not just for Nicole."

At the intense, undisguised yearning in his eyes, Clare's heart stopped, then raced on. And all he was doing to kindle that reaction was holding her hand. Gently. Tenderly.

Adam studied Clare. She hadn't pulled away from him, but he was well aware of her conflicting emotions: confusion, yearning, panic. The same things he was feeling.

Adam hadn't expected his birthday to end this way. He'd asked her to join him on the porch to see if he had the courage to begin the process of opening up. But he'd ended up sharing far more than he'd planned. Which was odd, considering how emotionally distant he'd always been. Yet he didn't feel distant from Clare, whose loveliness and goodness and strength had not only touched his heart, but refreshed his parched and weary soul.

It had been a long time since Adam had kissed a woman. There had been no one after Elaine. And he'd keenly felt the loss of that human connection. Sometimes the loneliness left him aching for something as simple as a gentle touch or a tender look. But he'd ruthlessly stifled such needs, knowing he didn't have the right stuff to sustain a long-term relationship, and unwilling to settle for less—or to hurt someone else by trying.

Yet Jack seemed to think he had changed, that he was now better able—or willing—to establish the kind of rapport that made a marriage not just work, but flourish. So did Clare, if he was reading her correctly. And he wanted to believe them. Desperately. Because he was tired of being alone. Tired of holding up the No Trespassing sign that blocked his heart. Tired of being cautious. And afraid. And second-guessing.

Adam knew he was heading toward shaky ground. That maybe he was being foolish, that he might regret his actions later. But right now, at this moment, with Clare only a whisper away, he didn't care. He needed her.

And so he decided to do something that could change their relationship forever.

Chapter Ten

Adam slowly reached over and touched Clare's face, tracing the elegant line of her jaw with a whisper touch. Her skin was just as he'd imagined it—silky and smooth and soft—and his mouth went dry as he struggled to get his heart rate under control.

Clare seemed to be faring no better. A pulse hammered in the delicate hollow of her throat, and he reassuringly stroked her hand—though he wasn't sure if that gesture was for his sake or hers.

Adam's fingers trailed from her cheek down the slender column of her throat, then around to the back of her neck. He cupped her head gently, and as he gazed into her deep-blue eyes, he signaled his intent, giving her a chance to pull away. When she didn't, he slowly, deliberately closed the gap between them and leaned down for a kiss.

When he finally broke contact his hands were trembling and he reached up to brush a stray strand of hair off her forehead.

"Are you okay?" he asked her unsteadily when he could find his voice.

She stared at him solemnly and blinked once. "I don't know."

He gave her a shaky grin. "Me, neither. Let's just sit for a minute, okay? I think we both need to regroup. Doctor's orders."

He kept one arm around her shoulder and pressed her head into the protective curve of his arm, letting his cheek rest against her silky hair.

Clare could hear the thudding of his heart against her ear. She knew her own heart was in no better shape. She wasn't quite sure what she'd anticipated from their kiss, but she hadn't expected it to leave her wanting more. She wasn't ready for more, though. And she wasn't sure Adam was, either. So where did they go from here?

As Adam held Clare, he had his own questions. Had he changed enough to make a relationship work over the long-term? Was he willing to trust his heart—completely—to another person? He'd shared a lot with Clare tonight. But it had been hard. Very hard. Opening up didn't come naturally to him, as it did to Jack. Could he sustain that kind of sharing long-term? Or would he eventually fall back into old patterns—and wind up hurting Clare?

He didn't know the answers to those questions. So as he stared at the blue-hazed mountains in the distance, he put the matter into greater hands.

Lord, please show me the way to proceed. I'm falling in love with Clare, and I'm not sure I can let her go when the nanny job is over. But I don't want to hurt her. Please help me to know Your will, to do the right thing. Help me to choose wisely and not make a decision that satisfies only my own selfish needs. Because as much as I want Clare in my life, I also want what's best for her. Even if that means letting her go.

"I wondered where you guys were."

At the sound of Nicole's voice, Clare abruptly straightened up and Adam withdrew his arm. She felt hot spots of color burning in her cheeks, and she averted her face on the pretense of arranging her sweater, feeling as guilty as a teenager caught necking in her parents' living room.

"I guess it's too late to play a game, huh?" Nicole said.

Clare risked a glance at Adam, wondering if he felt as embarrassed as she did. But if the twitch at the corner of his mouth was any indication, he seemed to find the whole thing humorous.

"Probably," he said. "Besides, I think you ladies should make an early night of it, considering all the hard work you did for my birthday."

"Yeah. And I still have some homework to finish."

"I'll be in to say good-night a little later."

"Okay. 'Night, Clare."

"Good night, Nicole. You did a great job on the party."

"Thanks." Nicole turned to go, but paused at the door to look back. "It's okay if you want to put your arm back around Clare's shoulder, Dad. I think it's kind of cool."

With that she disappeared inside, letting the screen door slam behind her.

Adam turned to Clare and chuckled. "So much for being discreet."

She gave him a wry look, her color still high. "Kids are smart. And attentive. They don't miss much. Listen, I'm sorry if this…well, I hope you weren't embarrassed."

"Not nearly as much as you were."

Nervously, Clare adjusted her sweater. "It's just that…well, I'm not sure I'm ready for anything…serious. I still have…issues."

"I do, too. And I've learned from experience not to rush

things. So let's just take this really slow, okay? I don't want anyone to get hurt."

She nodded and glanced toward the house. "Including Nicole. She and I have gotten pretty close, and she's asked me a couple of times about leaving. I don't want to build up any false hopes."

"I've thought about that, too," he replied. "I know she has a tendency to read too much into things sometimes. But I do agree with her about one thing."

"What?"

He draped his arm loosely around her shoulders and grinned. "I think this is kind of cool."

Clare smiled, but she didn't respond.

Because even though she didn't want to get her own hopes up, and even though she still had issues to resolve, she couldn't contain the glow that suddenly suffused her heart and spilled over, radiating warmth right down to her fingertips.

"Adam? I think you better take this call. It's the police."

Adam's head snapped up and he stared at Janice, who had just returned from maternity leave. "What?"

"It's the police. They said there's been…an accident. Line two."

Adam felt his heart stop, then race on as he glanced at his watch and reached for the phone. Clare was supposed to drive Nicole to a friend's house for a Friday-night sleepover about an hour ago. *Dear God, let them be okay!* he prayed.

He punched the number and tried unsuccessfully to speak, then cleared his throat and tried again. "This is Adam Wright."

"Dr. Wright, this is Lieutenant Stevens, Highway Patrol. Do you have a daughter named Nicole?"

"Yes."

"There's been a car accident. She's been taken to Memorial Hospital in Asheville."

Adam's grip on the phone tightened, turning his knuckles white. "How bad is it?"

"I wasn't at the scene myself. I only have a notation that it was a head injury."

Adam closed his eyes and tried to breathe. "What about Clare?" he asked hoarsely.

There was a sound of rustling paper. "I don't see anyone named Clare on the accident report. The driver was a Kathleen Foster. Her daughter, Jennifer, is also listed. They have minor injuries."

Adam frowned. "Are you sure?"

"That's what the report says."

"All right. Thanks. I'm on my way." Adam replaced the receiver, grabbed his briefcase and headed out the door. Janice gave him an anxious look as he strode past the desk, but he hardly paused, speaking over his shoulder in a clipped, rapid-fire tone.

"Cancel all my appointments for the rest of the day. I'm heading to Memorial Hospital in Asheville. Nicole was in a car accident. She has head injuries. And see if you can track down Clare. I'll call when I know something."

Adam didn't remember the drive to the hospital. All he knew was that he broke every speed law in the books. And that he prayed more fervently than he had in a long, long time.

When he reached the hospital, Adam parked his car illegally right outside the emergency room and almost ran inside. A woman who looked badly shaken, her arm in a sling, stopped him inside the door.

"Dr. Wright?"

He turned to her with an impatient frown. "Yes?"

"I'm Kathleen Foster. We met at the holiday concert at school. I'm so sorry about this." She was close to tears, and her face had an unhealthy pallor. "The truck crossed the median and I...I did the best I could."

Her voice broke, and despite his own panic, Adam shifted into doctor mode. "I'm sure you did. Look, Mrs. Foster, why don't you sit here for a few minutes?" He guided her to a chair. "I'm going to check with the doctor in charge. Is someone coming to be with you?"

She sniffed and nodded. "My h-husband is on his way. M-my daughter's still back there, but I w-wanted to catch you when you arrived."

"You just take it easy for a few minutes."

Adam left her, then made his way to the receptionist. "I'm Dr. Adam Wright. My daughter was in the car accident. I'd like to speak to the attending physician. Stat."

At his authoritative tone, the woman nodded and pressed a button, releasing the door to the emergency room. "Come in, please. I'll get her."

Sixty eternal seconds later, a tall, slender woman with short-cropped dark hair joined him inside the door and held out her hand.

"Dr. Wright? Ellen Grady. First, relax. I think your daughter will be fine. She hit the side of her head against the window when the car turned over, and she was unconscious for a few minutes. She's alert now, and there's no sign of serious trauma. Just a mild concussion, and some pretty colorful bruises on her right arm and leg."

Adam felt the coil of tension in his stomach ease slightly, and he wiped a shaky hand down his face. "Thank God!" he said hoarsely.

"Your daughter has been asking for you. But before I take you back, do you have any questions?"

He forced himself to take a deep breath, then slowly let it out before asking a series of concise, pointed questions to verify that the appropriate, comprehensive battery of tests had been performed. When he was satisfied, Dr. Grady led him down the hall to Nicole.

She was lying on an examining table in one of the small rooms, holding an ice pack against a rapidly discoloring bump on her right temple, her French braid in disarray. And she looked scared. Adam quickly moved beside her, reaching down to gently brush the hair back from her face.

"Hi, sweetie."

She reached out and grasped his hand tightly. "The truck was c-coming right at us, Dad," she said, her voice catching on a sob, her eyes still wide with terror. "I—I thought we were going t-to die."

He leaned down and pulled her slight, angular body close, burying his face in her hair. "It's okay, sweetie. Everything's okay now."

He held her for a long moment, and when she finally spoke again, her voice was muffled against his chest. "Can we go home now, Dad?"

"I think so. Sit tight and I'll check with Dr. Grady."

He found the woman in the hall outside, and she confirmed his assessment. "Normally I might want to keep her for observation, but you certainly know what to look for," she said. "And frankly, people are generally better off at home, anyway. I'll sign the release and you can be on your way. Someone will be in to help Nicole dress."

"Thanks. What about the others? I saw Mrs. Foster in the waiting room, with her arm in a sling."

Dr. Grady nodded. "Dislocated collarbone. Her daughter has a sprained ankle. According to the police, it's a miracle all three of them weren't killed."

"Is there someone who can tell me exactly what happened?"

The doctor snagged the sleeve of a passing aide. "Are any of the officers who came in with the car accident still here?"

The young man nodded. "There's one in the coffee room. I'll get him."

While Adam waited, the receptionist came over to him. "Mrs. Foster asked me tell you that she and her daughter went home, but she left her phone number if you want to call her." She held out a slip of paper.

"Thanks."

"Dr. Wright? Officer Parisi."

Adam turned and took the man's proffered hand. "My daughter was in the accident. Can you tell me what happened?"

"Near as we can tell, a truck in the oncoming lane lost control. The driver of your daughter's vehicle was alert and had good reflexes, so she was able to swerve out of the way and avoid a collision. Unfortunately, she slid off the edge of the highway and her vehicle fell onto its right side. It's pretty much totaled, but at least no one was badly injured." He shook his head. "This could have had a whole different ending if there'd been a head-on. Those three people were very lucky."

Adam didn't think it was just luck. But he let that pass. "Thank you, officer."

"My pleasure. I wish all of my calls ended this well."

Before he returned to the examining room, Adam stepped outside to phone Janice. After he gave her a quick update on the situation, he asked about Clare.

"I've been trying steadily since you left to reach her, but there's no answer at your house or in her apartment."

Adam frowned. "Okay. Thanks. Any urgent calls that I need to return?"

"Nothing that can't wait."

"All right. See you Monday."

As Adam rang off and made his way back to the examining room, his frown was still in place. Where was Clare? Kathleen Foster might know, but she was on her way home. That left only Nicole.

She looked up when he rejoined her and started to get off the table, but Adam moved swiftly beside her. "Hey, not so fast! You've got one big lump on that hard head of yours, and you might be a little dizzy."

She clung to him and closed her eyes when she stood. "Yeah," she said faintly.

Once he had her buckled into the car, he slid behind the wheel and backed out. As he edged into traffic he glanced over at her. She had her head back and her eyes were closed.

"Nicole?"

"Hmm?" she said sleepily.

"Do you know where Clare is?"

"Home, I guess," she mumbled.

He frowned. Not according to Janice. "Sweetie, why didn't she drive you to the party?"

Nicole didn't answer, and he glanced over. She'd snuggled into the corner, her lashes dark against her pale cheeks, and her even breathing told him that she was asleep. So he didn't disturb her with more questions. Because in less than forty-five minutes they'd be home. And he'd find his own answers.

Clare's car was in the garage.

As Adam set the brake on his own car, he frowned. She was obviously home now. But where had she been earlier? What had been so important that she couldn't take Nicole to the party?

As Adam carefully unbuckled his daughter and lifted her gently in his arms, his tension began to give way to anger. She'd suffered only minor injuries in the accident, but according to the officer, the outcome could have been far worse. Nicole could have been killed. His gut clenched painfully, and he had to blink rapidly to clear his suddenly blurred vision. When he thought how close he'd come to losing the daughter he was only just beginning to find…. His mouth settled into a grim line. Clare better have a rock-solid reason for putting his daughter's welfare into someone else's hands, he thought angrily.

As soon as Adam had Nicole settled in her room, he headed to the garage. He took the steps two at a time, then rapped sharply on the door. As he waited for Clare to answer, he tried to think of an excuse that he would consider acceptable. He couldn't come up with one, short of a death in the family.

He prayed that wasn't the reason.

But he knew that anything less would represent a betrayal of the trust he'd placed in her when he'd given her responsibility for the care of his daughter.

It was a no-win situation.

Someone was using a jackhammer in the next room.

Clare struggled to raise her heavy eyelids. No, it was the door, she realized. Someone was knocking on her door. Though pounding might be a better description, she thought with a groan, when the noise intensified. And it didn't sound as if they had any intention of going away.

With a supreme effort, she swung her feet to the floor and stood dizzily. Holding on to furniture for support, she made her way unsteadily to the door, where it took several fumbling tries before she managed to slide the lock back and pull it open.

Clare stared at Adam on the other side. At least she thought it was Adam. But she'd never seen that look on his face before. His eyes were cold and angry, and his mouth looked hard and tense. She tried to think clearly.

"Is something wrong?" she asked.

His eyes blazed. "Yes, something is wrong. Where have you been?"

"Here."

"You never left the apartment today?"

"No. I've been sleeping."

His frown deepened and his eyes grew even colder. "So there was no emergency?"

She stared at him blankly. "What?"

She saw a muscle twitch in his jaw. "Okay, look. I don't have time to discuss this now. But there's been a car accident. Nicole has a concussion. I brought her home from the hospital and I need to sit with her. We'll talk about this later."

He turned to go, and Clare clutched his sleeve, her eyes wide with shock. "Is she okay?"

Adam looked back at her. "No thanks to you," he said tersely. "She could have been killed. You said you were going to drive her, Clare. I counted on you. I didn't expect you to abdicate your responsibility and palm her off on Jennifer's mother."

Clare felt as if she'd been slapped. She recoiled slightly, her shoulders slumping as her eyes filled with tears. "Adam, I...I'm so sorry," she whispered. "Please...let me sit with her."

"I can take care of my own daughter," he said stiffly, his eyes like ice.

And with that he turned away and disappeared down the steps.

Slowly Clare closed the door, numb with shock. Tremors ran through her body, and she wasn't sure her wobbly legs would support her as she haltingly retraced her steps. But she didn't crawl back into bed. Instead, she opened her closet and reached for a small box on the shelf. She set it on the bed and, with shaky fingers, gently lifted the lid.

The photo she wanted was right on top, and for a moment she simply stared at it, tracing the edge of the frame with her finger. Dennis and David smiled back at her from the frozen moment in time, so achingly familiar, so much a part of her, so alive—and yet gone forever. She'd snapped the photo a couple of weeks before the accident that had cut their lives far too short.

The accident she'd caused.

Just like today.

As she lifted the photo, Clare's legs suddenly gave way and she sank to the floor. She put the photo against her chest and huddled into it, wrapping her arms around her body. She'd been here before. Felt the same crushing guilt. Over the past few months she thought she'd begun to deal with that burden, to gradually let it go. But now it came back, as sharp and intense and painful as ever. Thank God this ending had been different! But she could claim no credit for that. Once again, she'd shirked her duty and disaster had followed. Would she never learn?

For two long years, Clare had held her tears in check. But now they refused to be contained. For several moments they ran down her cheeks silently, and then a sob rose in her throat. And another. And still another. Until finally her body was wracked by them. Deep sobs filled with pain and regret and sorrow.

Clare had often felt alone since the accident. There had been times when the loneliness tunneled to the very depths of her soul, leaving her feeling hollow and empty. She didn't want to go there again, she thought in anguish. *Couldn't* go there again. Not if she wanted to survive.

Clare closed her eyes and rested her forehead on her knees. She desperately needed compassion. And kindness. And understanding. Thanks to Reverend Nichols, she'd found her way back to the ultimate source of all of those things. The One who didn't need words. Who could read what was in her heart and know what was needed.

And so Clare didn't even try to articulate the complexity of her emotions, the intensity of her distress, the depth of her despair. She just sent a simple, heartfelt plea.

Lord, I need You! Please help me!

With an effort, Adam forced his face to relax before he stepped into Nicole's room. But it wasn't easy. He was more angry than he'd ever been in his life. Clare had offered no explanation, no excuse for shirking her duty. He had trusted her with his most precious gift—his daughter—and she'd betrayed that trust. He found that hard to forgive.

Nicole looked at him when he entered the room. She was still far too pale, and the bump was now a garish purple, but the terror had faded from her eyes. He sat down on the bed and took her hand.

"How are you, sweetie?"

"My head hurts."

He reached into his pocket and pulled out a small penlight. "I'm not surprised. You might have a headache for a few days. Let's have a look at those pupils." He flashed the light in each eye, getting the response he hoped for. "Looking good. You just need to rest. I'll be close by."

She snuggled deeper into the bed and let her eyelids drift closed. But she opened them as he started to rise. "Dad? How's Clare?"

He looked down at her with a frown, wondering if her thinking was still a little muddled. "She wasn't in the accident, sweetie."

Nicole gave him an exasperated look. "I know that. She stayed here because she was sick. That's why Mrs. Foster took me. Is she okay?"

The twin furrows on Adam's brow deepened. Clare had finished her stint as a temporary receptionist the prior week, and he'd hardly seen her the past few days as he struggled to deal with an unusual spring outbreak of the flu. He tried to replay the encounter he'd just had with her, but he'd been so upset and angry that his powers of observation hadn't exactly been at their peak. Now that he thought about it, though, she had looked a little flushed. And her eyes…hadn't they seemed a bit dull and slightly unfocused?

"Dad?"

Nicole's voice brought him back to the present, and he reached down to give her hand a squeeze. "I'm going to run over there right now and check on her. I'll be back in a few minutes, okay?"

"Okay."

As Adam strode back toward the garage, a queasy feeling began to grow in the pit of his stomach—along with a growing certainty that he'd been way out of line, that he'd jumped to conclusions and wrongly berated Clare. After all these months, didn't he know her well enough to know that she'd never do anything to endanger Nicole? How could he have been so stupid? Even though he'd been upset about the accident and his nerves had been stretched to the breaking point, that didn't give him the right to take out his stress on the woman who had given him back his daughter in the first place.

Adam took the stairs two at a time, lifted his hand to knock—and froze. The muffled sound of raw, heartbreaking sobs came through the door, and he closed his eyes, feeling as if someone had kicked him in the gut. *God forgive me,* he prayed, his hands balling into fists.

Adam didn't even knock. He tried the door, found it open, and stepped into the dimness. The sound of Clare's anguished sobs led him to the bedroom, his stomach clenching more tightly with every step. And the sight of her huddled miserably on the floor, her head bent, her slight shoulders heaving, made him feel physically sick.

He went down on one knee beside her and laid a gentle hand on her shoulder. "Clare?"

She raised dull, bleary eyes to him, but it seemed to take a moment for his presence to register. She was clutching a picture frame to her chest. "I—I'm so s-sorry, Adam," she said hoarsely, repeating her earlier apology.

His drew a ragged breath. "I'm the one who's sorry." Then he reached for her and gathered her slender, shaking body into his arms.

Adam felt her misery at the deepest level of his soul, and the incoherent snatches of phrases that were interspersed with her sobs tore at his heart.

"My fault… Selfish… My responsibility… Accident… no…! Not gone…! Nicole, please… So alone…"

"Shh, it's okay, Clare. It's okay." He stroked her back gently and pulled her closer, his chin dropping to graze her forehead. But when his skin made contact with hers he quickly backed off in alarm and stared down at her. She was burning up! Her face was flushed, and not just from crying. He placed a cool palm against her fiery forehead and tried not to panic as he reached for her wrist to check her pulse. She had been trembling before, from emotion, but suddenly her whole body began to shake with bone-jarring chills.

"Clare." When she didn't respond, he tried again, more insistently. "Clare!"

She lifted her head and tried to focus on him.

"Clare, how long have you been sick?" he asked, speaking slowly.

"Since l-last night," she whispered hoarsely, her teeth chattering.

"Have you been throwing up?"

He wasn't surprised when she nodded. He'd treated enough cases to recognize the symptoms and instantly diagnose the problem. But this was one of the worst cases of flu he'd seen. She needed immediate—and constant—attention. And so did Nicole. Which meant there was only one solution.

"Clare, you have the flu," he said. "Since I have to care for both you and Nicole, I want you to come over to the house, okay?"

He wasn't quite sure she understood, but she nodded.

He reached over and pried her hands from the frame, glancing at the photo as he stood. And once more, he felt as if someone had delivered a punch to his stomach. The two smiling male faces in the photo had to be Clare's husband and son. The ones who'd been killed in a car accident. Just as Nicole almost had been today. He could only imagine the nightmare memories, and the pain, that today's scenario had evoked for the woman who now sat slumped at his feet. And his insensitive behavior had only made things worse.

He closed his eyes and bowed his head. *God forgive me,* he prayed again. *And please console Clare.*

Adam gently set the photo on the chest of drawers, then reached down and drew Clare to her feet in one smooth, easy motion. She wavered and gripped his arm, closing her eyes.

"I—I think I'm going t-to throw up again," she said faintly.

With Adam half carrying her, they made it to the bathroom just in time for her to be violently sick. When the retching finally stopped, she was so spent that she couldn't even stand without his support.

"I—I feel like I'm dying," she whispered miserably.

"Not if I can help it."

Adam guided her out of the bathroom, but when she stumbled he reached down and swept her up, cradling her against his broad chest. She was too weak to do more than lie passively in his arms.

"I'm sorry for the trouble," she whispered, her eyes huge in her pale face. Tears pooled in the corners of their blue depths, then spilled onto her cheeks. "It's all my fault."

Adam didn't know whether she was talking about the accident or about being sick. But it didn't matter. Neither was her fault—despite the blame he'd harshly laid on her during his first visit.

As he made his way carefully down the narrow staircase, Adam recalled that he'd asked God earlier to forgive him.

But as he looked down at the devastated face of the woman in his arms, he wasn't sure Clare ever would.

Chapter Eleven

The next twenty-four hours were a blur for Clare. She was alternately burning hot or freezing cold. Every muscle in her body ached. Her restless sleep was filled with heart-pounding nightmares that woke her abruptly, shaking and gasping for breath. And every once in a while something unpleasantly cold was insistently pressed to her chest.

But if she was aware of the bad, she was also cognizant of the good. The cool cloths on her forehead. The strong arm supporting her shoulders while she greedily drank great quantities of water. The gentle fingers massaging her aching muscles. And the soothing voice that always seemed to be there when she awoke from her bad dreams, reassuring and comforting her.

Clare lost all track of time. But when her eyelids flickered open after one of her frequent naps, she somehow knew she had turned a corner. Though she felt limp as a rag doll, her muscles no longer ached with such fierce intensity. Nor did she feel too hot or too cold. Just drained. And absolutely exhausted.

Clare turned her head toward the window, a simple action that seemed to require an extraordinary amount of energy. The shade was drawn, but faint light showed around the edges. Which meant it was either morning or evening. But she had no idea what day it was.

A movement on the other side of the room caught her eye, and she summoned up the energy to turn her head back in that direction. Nicole had cracked the door and was peeking in.

Clare managed a weak smile. And an even weaker greeting.

Instead of responding, Nicole turned and called out excitedly. "Dad! She's awake!"

A moment later Clare heard rapid footsteps on the stairs, and then Adam appeared in the doorway. "Wait out here," he instructed Nicole as he strode into the room. "I don't want to have to put you back on the patient list." He sat on the edge of the bed, then looked at Clare assessingly. Her eyes were clearer and more focused, and when he laid a hand on her forehead it was blessedly cooler.

As he reached for the stethoscope around his neck, Clare spoke. "You should warm that thing up before you use it. It's a form of torture."

Her voice was scratchy and almost unrecognizable, but he caught the faint teasing tone. For the first time in more than twenty-four hours, he felt the tension in his shoulders ease. "Welcome back," he said quietly. Following her advice, he warmed the stethoscope between his palms for a moment, then leaned over and slipped it inside the V-neck of her sweatshirt. "Just breathe when I tell you," he instructed.

While Clare followed his instructions, she assessed Adam. He looked as if he'd aged ten years, she realized with a pang. Twin furrows were etched deeply in his brow, and there were lines of tension and strain around his mouth and eyes. He looked utterly weary…and utterly wonderful, she thought, her throat contracting with emotion.

As he withdrew the stethoscope and looped it around his neck, fragments of the past twenty-four hours began to fall into place for Clare. "Adam…the accident… Is Nicole okay?"

He nodded. "The only remnants are a nasty bump on the head and some bruises."

"I'm so sorry," she whispered. "I should have…"

Adam silenced her by pressing a gentle finger to her lips. "This was not your fault, Clare," he said firmly. "If anyone should apologize, it's me. But you're in no condition right now to even think about everything that happened. You need to focus on getting well."

"What day is it?"

"Saturday night."

"And the accident was…"

"Yesterday, late afternoon. Now, I'm going to heat some soup and try to get something a little more solid into you. Do you need anything first?"

She blushed. "I…uh…need to go to the bathroom."

He nodded. "Good. Up till now, your body has been burning off the liquid almost as fast I could get it into you. If your fever hadn't dropped within the next couple of hours, I would have had to hospitalize you and get you hooked up to an IV."

She made a face. "Hospitals aren't my favorite place. No slight intended to your profession."

He smiled. "They're not my favorite place, either. I do everything I can to keep people out of them."

He rose and drew back the covers, then reached down

to help her sit up. "Take it slow and easy. Just let your feet
dangle over the side of the bed for a minute before you
try to stand."

Clare did as he advised, almost frightened by her ex-
treme weakness. "Wow!" she breathed softly. "This is
weird. I feel like every ounce of my energy has been
drained off and my muscles have gone on strike."

"A bad case of the flu will do that to you."

"But I never get sick! And I've never had the flu."

"You've never worked in a doctor's office before—especially one overflowing with flu patients. Trust me, you
just made up for all the years you escaped," he told her,
and though his voice was light she heard the serious un-
dertones. And knew she had been a lot sicker than she
could even imagine.

"Ready?" he asked. At her uncertain nod, he reached
down and eased her to her feet. She grasped his arm
tightly, then clung to him as he guided her slowly down
the hall and into the guest bath. "Can you manage on your
own?" he asked, giving her a worried look.

She nodded, not at all sure she could but equally sure
there was no acceptable alternative.

"Okay, I'll wait out here."

By the time she opened the door a couple of minutes
later, she had to hold on to it for support. Her legs had
grown wobbly, and her hands were shaking. "You'd think
I'd just run a marathon or something," she tried to joke,
but she was too weary even to smile.

Without giving her time to protest, Adam reached
down and tucked a hand under her knees, then swept her
into his arms. He grinned at her as he started back down
the hall. "I want you to know that I don't give this kind
of service to all my patients," he teased.

As Clare looked up at him, she was overcome by his kindness and tender care, and she felt tears leaking out the corners of her eyes. She tried to avert her face, embarrassed at her uncharacteristic loss of control, hoping Adam wouldn't notice.

When he reached the bed, he gently laid her down and tucked the covers around her. Then he sat beside her and tenderly traced the line of one tear down her cheek, dashing her hopes that she had successfully hidden them.

"It's okay to cry after all you've been through, Clare," he said softly. "When you're stronger, we'll talk. Right now, you just need to rest. Physically and mentally." He rose. "I'll get that soup."

As Adam disappeared out the door, Clare thought about his advice. She could easily comply with the instruction to get physical rest. She really didn't have much choice.

But she wasn't so sure about the mental part.

Because the feelings and emotions Nicole's accident had awakened were far too powerful to ignore. Even though she'd managed to suppress them for nearly three long years, she sensed that this time she'd have to deal with them.

Once and for all.

Clare's recovery took far longer than she expected. For the first few days she could hardly drag herself to and from the bathroom. By the end of the week she felt strong enough to get dressed, but even the smallest chores tired her out. Adele had been a huge help, bless her heart. She'd dropped off several home-cooked meals and had come to stay with Clare the first couple of days when Adam had to go back to work. Nicole had been equally attentive. All in all, Clare couldn't have asked for better care.

But even though everyone kept a close eye on her, she still had plenty of time alone, with nothing to do but pray. And think. About mistakes and guilt and grief. About how dramatically her life had changed nearly three years ago. And about how dramatically Adam's might have changed just a few days ago. Thanks to her.

Intellectually, Clare knew that the circumstances of this accident were different than the one that took the life of her husband and child. Her abdication of responsibility this time hadn't been brought about by selfishness, but by sickness. Yet the outcome could very well have been the same. And how could she have lived with that? How could she live with it even now, knowing what might have happened?

"I'm on my way to the hospital, but I called and found out the Bluebird has meat loaf today. How does that sound for dinner?"

Clare turned toward Adam as he joined her on the porch. He'd run himself ragged looking after her in addition to taking care of Nicole and keeping up with the demands of his practice. And it showed in his face. He looked worn out. Luckily it was Saturday and he'd have a chance to rest a little.

"Why don't I make something tonight?"

"Not yet."

"Adam, I'm not an invalid."

"Not yet," he repeated firmly. "Doctor's orders."

She sighed and let her head drop back against the wicker chair. "You're spoiling me."

When he didn't respond, she turned her head, and the expression in his eyes made her breath catch in her throat.

"Impossible," he said quietly.

She forced herself to look back at the mountains as her heart filled with tenderness for this special man. A man she wanted to spend the rest of her life with. A man she hoped felt the same way about her.

But first she needed to take care of some unfinished business. Because until she dealt with the debilitating grief and guilt locked inside, until she released them from her heart, there was no way for love to get in. And she wanted to let love in. She wanted to let Adam in.

She took a deep breath. "Adam…I need to go back to Kansas City."

When he didn't respond, she turned to look at him again. His eyes were guarded—but she saw fear lurking in their depths.

"I thought you were staying for three more weeks," he said carefully.

She gave him a startled look, realizing he'd misunderstood her intent. "I am!" she reassured him quickly. "I just have to…take care of some business."

"Then…you're coming back?"

"Of course." She saw the tension ease in his shoulders. "I'm sorry…I didn't mean to imply I was leaving for good."

He smiled, but it was clearly forced. "Good. I was afraid that maybe the medical care wasn't quite up to par."

"No one has ever taken such good care of me," she told him quietly.

After a long moment, Adam broke eye contact and glanced down at his watch. "I need to get rolling. As soon as I do rounds, I'll be back. Nicole is going to a barbecue, so I thought maybe you and I could eat out here. The weather's been great, and you can't beat the view!"

"That sounds lovely."

"Nicole is upstairs if you need her."

"I know. I'll be fine." When he hesitated, she smiled. "Really, Adam. I'll be fine. I'm feeling stronger every day."

He nodded slowly. "Okay. But don't get too ambitious. You're not back to full speed yet. When were you thinking of going back to Kansas City?"

"Next weekend."

He frowned. "That's a long trip."

"I'll take it slowly."

He hesitated. "I'm not sure you should go by yourself. Would you…like me to come with you?"

She looked at him in surprise, touched by his unexpected offer, but shook her head. "No. This is something I need to do alone. It will only take a couple of days. But thank you, Adam."

With a nod, he reentered the house to prepare for his hospital visit. But his mind wasn't on his patients. It was on Clare and her upcoming trip. She'd assured him that it would be a quick visit, and he believed her. But it reminded him that time was running out on the nanny assignment. In three short weeks Clare would be gone. Permanently.

Unless he gave her a very good reason to stay.

"I moved back into my apartment today."

Adam looked across the wicker table at Clare. He couldn't really argue about her decision. She was perfectly capable now of taking care of herself. But he would miss having her living under his roof. "I suppose it was time," he concurred.

"More than time. I was way too lazy way too long."

"You were very sick, Clare."

She toyed with her garlic mashed potatoes. "But I'm fine now."

He glanced down at her half-eaten dinner. "Your appetite still isn't back to normal."

"It's coming along."

"You can't afford to lose any more weight."

She couldn't deny that her clothes were starting to hang on her. "I'll gain it back."

Adam laid his fork down. "Clare, I'm still worried about you making this trip to Kansas City. I'm not sure you're strong enough."

"I will be by next weekend."

He expelled a frustrated sigh. "Is this something you have to do now? Can't it wait a little longer?"

She shook her head. "I need to go at that particular time, Adam."

The resolute look in her eyes told Adam that she wasn't going to be dissuaded. So he didn't argue. Besides, he had an even touchier subject to discuss with her. He reached for his iced tea and took a sip, trying to figure out how to begin. Clare didn't seem to harbor any ill will toward him since his insensitive treatment of her the day of Nicole's accident, but he'd learned enough since then to know that she should. As he'd held her, comforted her through countless fever-induced nightmares, he'd been able to piece together some details about the accident that had killed her husband and son. Enough to know that Clare blamed herself for their deaths. That she felt she'd reneged on her obligations and let them down.

Exactly the things he'd accused her of with Nicole.

None of which were true.

Just as he was sure they weren't true with her own fam-

ily. And he needed to convince her of that, to relieve her
of the torment that she still carried in her heart over that
accident. He had felt her deep-seated pain, and though
she'd hidden it well before her illness—as she was hid-
ing it well now—he knew it was still there. He wanted to
release her from that suffering and help her heart heal, just
as he'd helped her body heal.

"Clare, does your trip have anything to do with Dennis and David?" he asked carefully.

After a moment of silence, she nodded. "Yes."

He set his iced tea down and leaned over to capture her
delicate hand in his. "Tell me about it, Clare."

His sun-browned fingers were so strong, yet so gentle, she reflected. Just like the man. She drew a ragged
breath. If she harbored any hopes of creating a future
with Adam, he deserved to know about her past. Even if
he thought ill of her because of the terrible decision she'd
made on that fateful day nearly three years ago.

"You talked a lot about them when you were sick,"
Adam spoke again. "And I had the feeling that you somehow think you were responsible for their deaths."

There was a long moment of silence while she tried to
swallow past the lump in her throat. "I was," she finally
whispered.

"Why don't I believe that?"

She looked over at him, her eyes raw and bleak. "It's
true, Adam. If I hadn't been so selfish, they'd still be
alive."

"Tell me," he coaxed again, his own eyes gentle.

So she did, haltingly at first, then more quickly, until
finally the words came out in an almost incoherent rush.
And in among the cold, hard facts, she wove her feelings
of selfishness and guilt and pain and all the reasons why

she felt responsible for the tragedy that had cut short the lives of the two people she loved most and changed her life forever.

When she finished she took a deep breath. "I thought I was making progress, that I was learning to let go of the guilt," she said brokenly. "And then the accident happened with Nicole. She could have been... She could have died, Adam! And it would have been my fault!"

He reached over with his other hand and cocooned hers protectively in his warm clasp. He'd thought a lot about the accident, too. And had come to a completely different conclusion.

"Let me tell you something, Clare. If anyone should feel guilty about recent events, it's me. Because I think you *saved* her life. And all I did was berate you for it."

Clare gave him a confused look. "I don't understand. You were right to be angry. It was my responsibility to take care of Nicole."

"And that's exactly what you did."

She shook her head, as if to clear it. "I'm sorry. I must be missing something."

"You are. And here it is. After the accident, I spoke with an officer who was at the scene. He told me how fortunate it was that the driver of Nicole's car was alert and had good reflexes, because she was able to swerve out of the way and avoid a collision. He also said things could have turned out very differently if there'd been a head-on crash. Clare, that's exactly what might have happened if you'd been driving. You were so sick that your reflexes were sluggish at best. By using good judgment and asking Mrs. Foster to take Nicole, you might have saved her life. And your own."

Clare stared at him, then closed her eyes and drew a deep breath. *"Thank you, God!"* she whispered.

"I made that same prayer, once rational thought prevailed. And I also prayed that you would forgive me. Because you have every right to hate me for the way I treated you," Adam told her quietly.

Clare opened her eyes. "I never held it against you, Adam. I've been there," she said fervently. "I know what it's like to lose people you love. And to be angry at those responsible. Because that's the same feeling I have against myself, for what happened to Dennis and David." She paused, and her eyes filled with tears. "Maybe I made the right decision this time. But I didn't the last time. Because I was too selfish."

Adam stroked her hand. "May I tell you something, Clare? At worst, you made a mistake. You did something out of character. But it was the type of mistake that would normally have no consequences. We all make those kinds of mistakes every day. That's just being human. But selfish? Never."

"That's what Reverend Nichols said. But I can't seem to let go of the guilt," she said with a sigh. "That's what this trip to Kansas City is all about. I need to deal with it. To try and put it to rest. And to let myself grieve." She ran her finger down her iced-tea glass, the beads of moisture damp against her finger, like teardrops. "Do you know, until the night I got sick, I had never cried for them?" she said softly. "I couldn't. I was afraid that I'd break apart if I did. But now I know that there is a time for tears. And a time for mourning. I need to get past the grief and the guilt so my soul can start to heal. Otherwise I'll never be able to move on. May fourteenth is...is the third anniversary of the accident. That's why I want to go back then."

Adam drew a deep breath. "I hate for you to have to deal with this alone."

She looked at him with quiet confidence. "I won't be alone, Adam. Thanks to Reverend Nichols, I've reconnected with the Lord. He'll be with me. But I could use your prayers."

"That goes without saying." He paused and squeezed her hand. "We'll miss you."

"I'll miss you, too. But I'll be back to finish out my assignment."

For the last three weeks.

The words were unspoken, but they hung in the air between them.

As Adam picked up his fork once more, he mulled over Clare's decision. She had made it clear that she was trying to tie up the loose ends of her old life so she could move on to a new one. By courageously confronting old demons, she was making a conscious effort to let go of the past so she could embrace the future with hope and peace.

Adam knew how hard that was. And he knew something else, as well.

The ball was now squarely in his court.

Clare stepped out the door of the motel into the blazing sun and almost recoiled from the hot, humid air that hit her in the face. Over the past few months she'd grown accustomed to the cooler climate in the mountains of North Carolina, and the unrelenting heat of Kansas City was a shock to her system. If it was already this bad at only nine-thirty in the morning, she knew it would surely be a sauna later in the day.

Resolutely, Clare straightened her shoulders. She wasn't going to let a little heat change her plans. Nor a little tiredness. Okay, maybe more than a little tiredness, she conceded. She'd assured Adam that she felt completely up to the trip, but the long drive had taken far more out of her than she wanted to admit. Though she'd tried to sound bright and perky when she'd called him last night to let him know she'd arrived safely, he'd seen through her pretense immediately, quickly discerning the underlying note of weariness in her voice. His own voice had been laced with worry when he'd spoken to her.

"Clare, I want you to get something to eat and go to bed. And promise me you'll sleep late tomorrow."

She'd been too tired to argue. "I will, Adam."

"And don't push yourself."

"I won't."

His sigh of frustration came clearly over the line. "I wish I was there."

"I know, but I need to do this alone."

"You also need to take care of yourself."

"That's exactly why I'm here, Adam."

"I mean physically."

"I'll do that, too."

There was a slight hesitation. "All right. I'll pray for you, Clare."

She replayed his promise in her mind as she locked the door of her motel room and headed for her car. She was going to need his prayers, she thought grimly. As well as her own.

Please, Lord, help me get through this. Let me feel Your steady, healing presence throughout this day. Give me the strength to confront the past and put it to rest.

Clare had carefully mapped out her route. Each place represented a significant part of her old life, starting with the house she had shared with Dennis and David.

As she pulled up across the street from the brick Colonial and put the car in Park, she let her gaze trace the contours of the stately home. The basketball hoop Dennis had installed was still visible above the side-entry garage, she noted, and a wistful smile tugged at the corners of her mouth as she pictured him unwinding after a long day by shooting baskets and, later, showing David how to play.

As she shifted her attention to the front of the house, she thought about the day Dennis had first brought her to see it, recalling the excitement in his eyes as he showed her around. Though she'd been suitably impressed, she'd found her greatest joy not in the house, but in the happiness it had given him.

She took a moment to replay in her mind the day they'd moved in. Dennis had insisted on carrying her over the threshold, and then they'd eaten a picnic dinner on the floor in the bare dining room while he described what the room would someday look like, promising to fill it with beautiful furnishings. A promise he had proudly kept.

When she looked at the window of the second-floor master bedroom her throat constricted with emotion. That room had been filled with love and laughter and sharing—a sheltered, special place where time stopped and the fears and concerns of the world disappeared.

David's room wasn't visible from the street, but she could picture it in her mind. Cluttered, filled with little-boy treasures like rocks, an occasional multilegged creature in a glass jar and shelves of soccer trophies. It had been right next to the master bedroom, and sometimes she and Dennis would stand in the doorway late at night, hand in hand, watching as David slept—and dreaming of the day when other childish voices, other childish treasures would fill the remaining empty bedrooms.

It was a dream that had never come true.

Clare blinked rapidly and swiped a hand across her eyes. She let her gaze once more sweep lovingly over the house and tucked the memory carefully in her heart. Then, with a final lingering glance, she drove away.

Her next stop was Dennis's office. She'd only gone inside the modern, mostly glass building a couple of times, when she'd met him for lunch. Today she remained in her car, looking at it from across the street, counting the floors until she could pick out the window of his spacious, tenth-floor office, with its commanding view of the city. Clare knew what that space represented to him. Beating the odds. Overcoming his background. Proving that he had the right stuff to succeed in a competitive, high-stakes world. Right or wrong, his success had helped him feel more worthy somehow. It had validated him. As a man of strong faith, Dennis had tried to keep worldly achievements in perspective. But he had still relished his success. Clare had understood that, given the poverty of his youth. And when she'd seen him here, in this world she only shared vicariously, she had been happy for him.

Her next stop was David's school. She didn't drive in, but stopped at the entrance gates. Which was where she had typically left him in the morning. He'd gotten to that age where having his mother drive him right to the door wasn't cool anymore. But she'd always waited while he walked up the curving driveway. And sometimes, as he'd trudged along, his knapsack slung over his back, she'd think ahead, to the day when life would take him much farther from her arms than a simple walk to the school door. She had wondered, back then, how she would cope when that time came, when she had to set him free to test his wings in the world. And she'd always dreaded that day.

She'd give anything now if she still had that to look forward to.

Struggling to contain her tears, she drove to the house where she'd attended the pool party. She hadn't known the host very well, but the party had been for a good friend of hers from her teaching days and she'd ended up having a wonderful time. The rambling, contemporary home on the corner lot looked exactly the same, she thought, as she slowly pulled to a stop. The pool was clearly visible behind a decorative iron fence, and though they weren't in use today, the lounge chairs were arranged much as they had been the day of the party. She'd been sitting in one along the far edge of the pool when the hostess had sought her out, portable phone in hand.

Clare had known right away that something was wrong from the expression on the woman's face. As she'd taken the phone, alarm racing up her spine, her heart had begun to thump heavily in her chest. And as she'd listened to the officer on the other end, who had apparently tracked her down from the pool party number Dennis had scribbled on a scrap of paper and tucked in his pocket in case he needed to reach her, she'd felt as if she'd been sucked into a vacuum, the party sounds fading away, the scene distorting before her eyes.

After that she'd switched to autopilot. She'd thrown a cover-up over her suit, and someone had driven her to the hospital. But it was already too late. Dennis had died at the scene. David had lingered briefly, but by the time she arrived at the hospital he was gone, too. All because she stayed too long at the party.

Clare hadn't been near a swimming pool since.

And she wasn't sure she would ever go to one again.

As she struggled to contain her tears, Clare realized

that her hands were shaking. It was well past noon, and she knew she should stop and rest. Maybe get some lunch. Adam would insist on it if he were here. But the thought of food made her queasy. And with the most difficult part of her day still ahead, rest wasn't an option. So she resolutely headed for her next stop.

The church she and Dennis and David had regularly attended was just as she remembered it, Clare noted, as she pulled into the adjacent parking lot. It had been almost a year since she'd set foot inside, and she prayed it would be open.

Luck was on her side. The door was unlocked, and Clare quickly understood why when she entered. There had obviously been a wedding a short time before. White bows still adorned the pews, and beautiful flower arrangements stood on the altar, filling the air with a sweet, fresh fragrance. She slipped into a pew near the back, letting the peace and beauty seep into her soul.

As she looked around the familiar interior, it struck her how many pivotal moments in life were celebrated in this holy place. The moments that mattered the most, if one took the eternal view. People came here to celebrate birth into new life through baptism. They came to celebrate the union of a man and woman in marriage. They came on Christmas to celebrate the birth of Christ—God's great gift to humanity. And on Easter, to commemorate His glorious resurrection, which forever destroyed the power of death. Finally, they came at the end of an earthly life to mark the transition to eternal life. People came here for so many important events.

But they also came for personal reasons. To seek solace. And guidance. And grace. They came to share with the Lord their sorrows. Their joys. Their uncertainties. In other words, they came to pray. Not necessarily in a formal way. But in conversation. Or, as Reverend Nichols had so simply put it, they came to talk to the Lord.

Clare closed her eyes and took a deep, steadying breath.

Lord, please help me to know Your forgiveness. Please relieve me of the burden of my grief. Help me to fully and completely put my life in Your hands, confident that You will show me mercy and understand my sorrow and regret. I need to move on, Lord. I need to let go of the past. But I need Your help to do it, once and for all. Please help me, so that I can find the peace that comes from total surrender to Your will. And please help me as I make this last, most difficult part of my journey. Please be by my side.

She lingered for a few more minutes in the peaceful refuge, drawing strength from its tranquility. But finally she rose. It was time.

She made just one brief detour, at a florist, on the way to her final destination. She hadn't mapped out this last leg of her trip, but even though she'd only been to the cemetery once, the route was etched indelibly on her mind.

As she slowly drove through the entrance, her last trip here came back with startling intensity. She recalled glancing out the window when the limo turned into the gates, noting the long line of cars behind her. The church had been packed, and apparently many had chosen to come to the graveside service, as well. A.J. and Morgan had sat on either side of her, gripping her hands tightly throughout the service and now, again, in the car. They hadn't spoken much. But their very presence, and the look in their eyes, had told her how much they cared, how deeply they grieved for her. She couldn't have made it through those terrible days without her sisters.

Clare pulled to a stop at the curb and reached for the flowers. She recognized the headstone, about twenty yards away, from the picture in the catalogue at the monument company. Slowly she got out of the car and forced her feet to move toward it. As she approached, the names on the stone gradually came into focus. Seeing them etched in granite, so permanent, so final, caused her breath to lodge in her throat, making it difficult to breath.

Dennis J. Randall. Beloved Husband.
David L. Randall. Cherished Son.

Then the dates…indicating lives cut far too short.
And finally, the Bible verse she had chosen.

For He has freed my soul from death, my eyes from tears, my feet from stumbling. (Ps 114: 8)

The words began to swim before Clare's eyes, and she sank to her knees beside the headstone, then dropped back on her heels. Unsteadily she reached over and let her fingers run lightly over the names, feeling the ridges and the valleys of the letters and the smooth, polished granite in between. The afternoon sun beat down on the back of her head and threw the letters into relief, each name casting a shadow that extended beyond the actual letters. Just as their lives extended beyond the grave, she thought. Dennis and David would always live in her heart, in a special place reserved only for them, cherished and loved for all time. And they would always live in heaven, in the loving care of the Lord.

Clare let one hand rest on top of the headstone, and with the other she reached for the flowers she'd set on the ground beside her. Tears began to roll down her cheeks, but she made no attempt to stop them. Not this time. Carefully she laid a red rose, then a yellow one, on the grave. One for love, one to say she would never forget them. The age-old language of flowers.

"I came today to say goodbye," she whispered, her voice choked. "And to say I'm sorry. To ask your forgiveness. To tell you that there hasn't been one day in the past three years that I didn't wish I could turn back the clock and make a different decision. I miss you both so much! When you left, the sunlight went out of my world. Everything turned dark, and I lost my way. I existed, but I didn't live. I knew that wasn't what God wanted for me, but I couldn't find my way back to the light."

Her voice caught on a sob, and she took a steadying breath. "Then, through Aunt Jo, God gave me a job to do. I've been trying to help a father and daughter create the kind of family we had. And I think I've succeeded. But something else happened along the way. I began to realize that I wanted to be part of their family. I knew I couldn't do that, though, until I made my peace with you. And until I grieved. That's why I came today. To tell you how much I love you. How much I'll always love you. And to tell you that just because I want to let other people into my heart, they will never take your place. There's a special spot that will always be reserved just for you."

She rested her cheek against the stone, and her tears made dark splotches on the polished surface. "I wish I could talk with you, could know for sure that you forgive me and that you're okay with me moving on. But I'll just have to trust that you know what's in my heart, and that you understand."

Slowly she slipped the ring off her left hand and carefully tucked it in her purse. Then she let her fingers once more lovingly caress their names. "Goodbye, my loves," she whispered.

For several minutes Clare remained in that position, the tears running freely down her face. Healing, cleansing tears of grief. Of closure.

When at last she straightened up, drained and weary, she was startled to find a cardinal staring at her from the ground, a few feet away. Oddly, the bird didn't seem a bit frightened by such close proximity to a human. Its scarlet head was cocked to one side as it regarded her quizzically. When Clare didn't move, it hopped a bit closer. Then closer still. There was something in its beak, but she couldn't quite make out what it was.

All of a sudden, the bird hopped onto the grave, dropped its cargo, then lifted its wings and soared into the air. Clare watched, mesmerized, as it rose against the clear blue sky, circled once and disappeared among the trees.

When she looked down, the bird's offering lay next to the roses she had placed there. Curiously she reached for it and set it in her palm. For a moment she couldn't figure out what the triangular object was. One edge was ragged, as if it had been torn, and what looked like part of a number was visible. She turned it over...and her breath caught in her throat.

A large heart filled the small piece of cardboard.

It was the corner of a playing card.

Clare wasn't a great believer in heavenly signs or messages from beyond the grave. But as she stared down at the sliver of cardboard in her hand, a profound, abiding peace spread throughout her. And in the deepest recesses of her soul, she felt as if she'd been given two precious gifts.

Absolution.

And permission to move on.

Tears once more filled her eyes, and she raised her face toward Heaven. "Thank you," she whispered.

Chapter Twelve

"It sure is quiet around here without Clare."

Adam's hand stilled for a moment, then he continued dishing out the Chinese food he'd brought home for dinner.

When he didn't respond, Nicole looked over at him. "Don't you miss her, too, Dad?"

He handed her a plate. "Yes. But she'll be back tomorrow."

Nicole sighed and glanced disinterestedly at her food. "Yeah, but not for long. She'll be leaving in two weeks. For good."

Adam was well aware of Clare's impending departure. It had been on his mind constantly. He'd prayed about it, asked for guidance, listened to his heart. He knew what he *wanted* to do. But he still wasn't sure it would be fair to ask Clare to commit to a man who had major problems with intimacy. Yes, they'd already connected and communicated on a deeper level than he ever had with Elaine. But could he sustain that? Or would he end up disappointing Clare? He didn't know the answer to that question. And he wasn't sure how to find it.

He'd struggled with another question, as well. He knew Nicole had come to care deeply about Clare. But was she ready to have someone move into a mother's role? Or would she resent another woman trying to take the place of the mother she had loved? Adam had been wanting to bring the subject up with Nicole for weeks, but he'd never found the opportunity. Or the courage. But time was running out. And there would be no better opportunity than now.

Adam forced himself to take a steadying breath and made a pretense of eating. "You're going to miss Clare, aren't you?" he asked, striving to keep his tone casual and conversational.

Nicole sighed. "Big-time. She's cool. I kind of hoped…"

Her voice trailed off, and Adam looked over at her. "Hoped what?" he prompted.

She shrugged. "I don't know. You put your arm around her once, out on the porch. And I see the way you guys look at each other, usually when you think the other one isn't watching. I'm not a kid anymore, you know. I thought maybe…well, that maybe you and Clare might fall in love or something. If you guys got married, she could stay."

Adam stared at her, stunned. "You hoped we'd get married?"

Nicole flushed. "Yeah."

"But…what about your mom?"

"What about her?"

"Well, I wasn't sure how you'd feel about someone taking her place."

Nicole shrugged unconcernedly. "Clare wouldn't do that. Clare is…Clare. She and Mom are a lot different. I love them both."

Adam stared at his daughter. She had honed right to

the essence of the situation, which he had obviously made far too complicated. And he couldn't argue with her logic. Elaine and Clare *were* different. Completely.

"So are you going to?" Nicole asked.

"What?"

"Ask her to marry you?"

He hesitated. "I don't know," he said slowly.

She tilted her head and studied him. "How come you're not sure?"

Because I don't want to hurt her. Because I'm still not convinced I'm husband material. Because I'm scared she'll say no.

But his spoken words were different. "I don't know if she loves me."

Nicole rolled her eyes. "Good grief, Dad! How can you be so dense! Of course she loves you!"

"How do you know?"

"I told you. I see the way she looks at you."

"Could you be a little more specific?"

"You know. Her eyes get kind of…soft or something. Like she thinks you're really special."

"Yeah?"

"Yeah. So are you going to ask her?"

"I guess I will."

Nicole grinned. "Cool! Then she can move into the house and we can be a real family."

As Nicole attacked her meal with sudden enthusiasm, her last words echoed in Adam's heart.

A real family.

That had a nice sound. A hopeful sound. And he wanted it more than he could say.

He just prayed Clare felt the same way.

* * *

"You didn't have to go to the Bluebird, Adam. I would have been happy to make dinner."

Adam glanced over at Clare. Since her return from Kansas City a few days before, she'd seemed tired and a bit too pale. He'd known the trip would take a lot out of her, physically and emotionally, and he'd been right. So he'd insisted that she take it easy for a couple of days.

"You can cook tomorrow if you really want to."

"I really want to."

She turned to look at the mountains then, and as he studied her in the twilight, he was grateful to see that tonight there was more color in her cheeks. She hadn't talked much about her trip, except to say that she was glad she had gone. But in her eyes there was a quiet serenity that hadn't been there before. And he had noted the absence of her wedding ring. So he knew the trip had done what she'd hoped—released her from the past so that she could build a new future.

A future he hoped included Nicole and him.

Adam felt his heart begin to thud heavily in his chest and he turned to look out over the distant mountains. He'd been waiting for the right moment to propose, and this seemed to be it. It was a beautiful evening, the stillness broken only by the song of birds. Nicole had gone to dinner at a friend's house and wouldn't be home until much later. It was the perfect time.

Adam swallowed and looked over at Clare. She was still focused on the mountains, her face placid and at peace, her legs curled up under her. She looked so right sitting there on his porch, he thought. As though she belonged with him. For always.

He cleared his throat, and Clare glanced at him expectantly. Suddenly he wished he was sitting beside her instead of in the wicker chair at a right angle to the settee. But maybe this was better. From here, he had a better view of her face, a better angle from which to gauge her reactions.

"We missed you while you were gone," he began.

"I missed you both, too."

"Nicole said it just wasn't the same around here without you."

A smile tugged at the corners of her mouth, but she remained silent.

"She was right," he added.

Again, Clare remained silent, her eyes inviting him to continue.

Adam leaned forward and clasped his hands between his knees. "The thing is, Clare, we don't want you to leave when the nanny job is over."

She waited a moment, as if she expected him to say more. When he didn't, she spoke. "I have a job waiting for me in Kansas City."

"But there's a job for you here, too."

The tiniest frown creased her brow. "I never planned to be a nanny permanently, Adam."

"I don't mean that job." He sighed and raked his fingers through his hair. "I'm sorry. I'm really making a mess of this. I've never been good at this kind of thing."

"Just tell me what's in your heart, Adam," she encouraged softly.

He looked over at her, suddenly afraid. Afraid to do as she asked. And just as afraid not to. If he told her what was in his heart, he would be completely vulnerable. But if he didn't, how could he convince her to stay? He fought against his doubts, but fear knotted his stomach and made it difficult to breathe.

When he spoke, his voice was taut with tension. "I'd like you to stay, Clare. As my wife."

For a long moment she searched his eyes. Then she spoke. "Why?"

It was a simple question. And the answer should be equally simple. But he couldn't say the words he knew she wanted to hear.

"I'd like us to be a family," he said unevenly. "You've been wonderful with Nicole, and she doesn't want you to leave. Neither do I. I think we could have a good life together, the three of us."

He knew his response was lame. He knew it even before he saw the flicker of hope that had initially sprung to life in her eyes change to disappointment, then to sad resignation. Nevertheless, she waited silently for a moment, giving him a chance to say something else. But he couldn't find the words.

Finally she spoke again. "Thank you for the offer, Adam," she said quietly. "But I'm not in the market for that kind of job. You and Nicole will be fine now. I've done what Aunt Jo asked me to do. It's time to move on."

Adam felt something inside him break.

Once more she waited. But when he didn't speak, she rose and looked down at him, her eyes sad—and hurt. "I'm pretty tired, Adam. I think I'll go back to my apartment and turn in early."

A moment later he heard the screen door close gently but firmly behind him.

Adam let his head drop into his hands. *Lord, what am I to do now?* he pleaded desperately in the silence of his heart. *I can't let Clare leave. She means more to me than life itself. Please help me find a way to convince her to stay. Give me the courage to fully open my heart to this special woman, to overcome my father's bitter legacy once and for all. Please give me another chance!*

Suddenly the words of Reverend Nichols's Easter homily came back to Adam. The minister had said that in order to grow, we have to be willing to trust our heart with other people. That unless we let go of our fear, we can never move forward or fulfill God's plan for us. And that we need to love as Christ did—completely, selflessly and without reservation.

Adam believed that in his heart. But putting it into action required tremendous courage. A courage he was afraid he didn't have.

"Dad? What's wrong?"

Adam lifted his head from his hands and looked up at Nicole from the shadows. He wasn't sure how long he'd sat on the porch, but the sky had grown dark.

Nicole moved closer. At the sight of his face, her eyes widened in alarm. "Is Clare sick again?"

Adam forced himself to straighten up. "No. She just went to bed early."

"So what's wrong?"

Adam sighed. "Sit down a minute, sweetie."

Nicole moved to the spot on the settee that Clare had vacated earlier and perched on the edge. When Adam didn't immediately speak, she leaned forward impatiently. "Dad?"

He wiped a hand wearily down his face. "Remember what we talked about the other night? About Clare staying? I asked her tonight. She said...no."

Nicole stared at him incredulously. "You asked her to

marry you?" At his nod, she frowned. "But she loves you!
What did you say to her?"

"I asked her to stay. As my wife."

Nicole's frown deepened. "What else?"

"I told her that I wanted us to be a family, and how
much she meant to you, and that we didn't want her to
leave."

She waited, much as Clare had waited earlier, as if expecting him to say more. When he didn't, Nicole leaned
forward. "Is that it?"

"Pretty much."

Nicole rolled her eyes. "That is so unromantic! It
makes it sound like the only reason you want her to stay
is because of me."

"But that's part of it," he said defensively.

She looked at him with a wisdom far beyond her eleven
years. "Dad, no woman is going to marry a guy because
his kid likes her."

Adam felt his neck grow red. "It's more than that."

"Than what?"

"I like Clare."

"*Like?*" she practically shrieked.

"Okay, okay. I love her."

"And…"

"And what?"

"Come on, Dad! What else? Tell me how you feel
about her." When he hesitated, she leaned over and laid
her hand on his knee. "It's okay. You can tell me. This is
the kind of stuff you share with people you love," she said
gently.

Adam drew an unsteady breath, digging deep for the
courage he hoped was there. "I—I can't imagine my life

without her anymore," he said quietly, his voice slightly unsteady.

"That's better," Nicole said encouragingly. "Keep going."

"Sometimes…sometimes it scares me, but the fact is…I need her. Because she makes me a better person. And she makes my life so much richer. When she walks into the room, it's like…like the sun coming out after a gray, rainy day. Everything seems so much better and brighter. I love her so much sometimes that…that it hurts."

There was silence for a moment, and when Adam risked a glance at Nicole she was staring at him in awe.

"Wow!" she breathed. "Did you say any of that to Clare?"

"Not exactly."

Nicole leaned forward. "You need to use those exact words, Dad! Man, she'll melt!"

"But she already said no, Nicole."

"So? You can't give up! But the next time you need to do this right. The words are important, but you also need to be more romantic."

Adam gave her a helpless look. "Romance isn't my specialty."

She dismissed his comment with a wave of her hand. "I have lots of ideas," she said confidently. "Do you want to hear them?"

Adam was pretty sure he wouldn't be very comfortable with Nicole's suggestions. But he didn't have any other brilliant ideas. And if she could help him figure out a way to change that look of sad resignation in Clare's eyes to one of love and acceptance, he was willing to give them a try. "I guess I don't have anything to lose at this point."

Nicole leaned forward eagerly. "Okay. Let's start with roses…."

* * *

Clare sat cross-legged on her bed, sorting half-heartedly through a box of printed material she'd accumulated since arriving in North Carolina. School schedules and phone numbers and driving directions and brochures about various points of interest in the area that she thought might someday make nice outings. She really didn't need any of it now, she thought, her spirits drooping.

Clare rested her chin in her hands and propped her elbows on her knees. This wasn't the way she'd hoped her time in North Carolina would end, she thought with a melancholy pang. Thanks to Aunt Jo, she had found a new family to love—and a wonderful man to spend the rest of her life with. She'd dealt with her guilt and her grief. She was ready to move on. To start a new life.

Unfortunately, the wonderful man wasn't.

Clare sighed. She knew that Adam loved her. Knew that his feelings for her ran deep and strong. But she also knew that unless—or until—he was able to express those feelings, to admit that he loved her and needed her just as much as she loved and needed him, the relationship would be out of balance. A marriage in which one party held back, withholding trust at the deepest level, was not the kind of marriage she wanted.

Clare knew that Adam's demons were powerful. That his father's legacy had made it difficult for him to show emotion, to let people get close. But she had thought that over the past few months he had begun to overcome that hurdle, to trust her enough to share what was in his heart.

Unfortunately, she'd been wrong.

And as much as she loved Adam, as much as she wanted to be part of this family, she wasn't willing to settle for anything less than a marriage in which both spouses shared fully in each other's lives—their joys and sorrows, doubts and hopes, dreams and fears.

And Adam wasn't there yet.

Maybe he would never be.

The sharp ring of the telephone interrupted that disheartening thought, and Clare padded to the kitchen to pick it up.

"Clare, it's Nicole. Are you busy?"

"Not really. Just going through some papers. What's up?"

"I was going to make some chocolate chip cookies, but I can't get the mixer to work."

"I thought we agreed you wouldn't do any baking unless I was there."

"I know. But you're leaving soon, and I need to figure out how to do it by myself."

"Is your dad around? Maybe he can look at the mixer."

"He's busy. I don't want to bother him."

Clare frowned. Adam had called earlier and left a message with Nicole that he wouldn't be home in time for dinner, and not to wait. So Clare had left him a plate in the oven. She'd heard him pull in about an hour ago, but he must be tied up with some emergency.

"Okay. I'll be right over."

Clare shoved her feet into a pair of canvas shoes and tucked her T-shirt into her jeans. She'd already taken her hair down for the night, so she simply ran a brush through it. This shouldn't take long.

She ran quickly down the narrow stairs. But when she opened the outside door at the bottom, prepared to dash over to the house, she pulled up short, her eyes widening in surprise.

At her feet lay a single long-stemmed red rose.

With a note attached.

Slowly Clare reached down and lifted the fragile blossom, letting her fingers trace the outline of the velvety petals. She looked around. There was no one in sight, but a flutter of the kitchen curtains told her Nicole was in on this. She glanced back down at the rose and flipped open the folded sheet of paper that was attached to the stem.

"Dear Clare, I have never been very good with words or expressing what's in my heart. Last night is just the latest dismal example. I know I can never make up for botching what should have been a beautiful moment between us. But at least I can try. If you can find it in your heart to give me one more chance, please follow the trail of roses. I'll be waiting at the end to meet you. The next rose is at the end of the driveway. Yours always, Adam."

Clare read the note a second time, then carefully folded it and slipped it into the pocket of her jeans. She tried to remain calm, to tell herself this might be another false start that would end just as badly as the first one. But somehow her heart wasn't listening. A buoyant sense of hope welled up within her, and she lifted the rose to her face to inhale its sweet, intoxicating fragrance.

"Thank you, Lord!" she whispered.

Slowly she made her way down the driveway, the gravel crunching beneath her feet in the stillness of the twilight. And just as Adam had promised, another rose lay at the end, pointing to the right.

Clare picked it up and continued her journey, following the quiet country lane until she came to another rose, which pointed down a barely visible, overgrown footpath that veered off into the woods. She picked that one up as well and set off down the path.

Clare had never been this way before. The path was on

private property, so she'd never explored it. And in the rapidly deepening dusk it was harder and harder to see the trail markings. But whenever she began to wonder if she had lost her way, she came upon another rose, confirming that she was still on the right track.

Clare counted the roses as she picked them up, and as she reached for the eleventh one she realized that it was pointing away from the path. With a frown she straightened and peered into the twilight. In the distance she could see a faint, indistinct glow, and she set off in that direction, weaving in and out among the trees.

When at last Clare emerged from the forest, her eyes widened in wonder at the enchanting scene before her. A white lattice arbor stood in a small, moss-covered clearing, backed by a clear, placid jewel of a lake. Inside the arbor were two chairs and a tiny table, draped with white linen. A plate of chocolate-covered strawberries stood in the center of the snowy expanse, with two crystal goblets beside it. The romantic strains of a classical string quartet drifted softly through the air. And there were candles. Dozens of candles. On the table. On the ground. Beside the lake. On stones and tree stumps and fallen logs. Illuminating the scene with golden, ethereal light.

It was magic.

But most magical of all was the man. Adam stood beside the arbor, impeccably dressed in a dove-gray suit, white shirt and silver-flecked tie. He was holding the final rose and gazing at her with an expression that could only be described with one word.

Adoring.

Clare melted.

For a moment the world stopped as their gazes connected. Clare saw in Adam's eyes exactly what she had always hoped to see. Love. Absolute, complete, unguarded love. He was holding nothing back.

Slowly she moved forward, until she was only a whisper away from him. He handed her the final rose, then lifted her hand to his lips.

Clare's throat constricted with emotion, and she felt tears of joy sting her eyes. Even though Adam hadn't yet said a word, she knew that the setting he had created tonight—with help from Nicole, she suspected—had taken him way out of his comfort zone. And gave her hope that he had, at last, found the courage to escape the bitter legacy of his father.

Adam saw the glimmer of tears in Clare's eyes and reached over to gently lay his palm against her cheek.

"I didn't plan to make you cry," he said huskily.

She blinked, then reached up to wipe the back of her hand across her eyes. "Adam, this is…" She gestured around the setting. "I can't even…" Her voice choked, and she had to stop and take a deep breath. "It's like something out of a storybook."

"When a man is blessed with a second chance to ask the woman he loves to marry him, he wants to do it right."

He took her hand and led her to one of the small white chairs, then gently urged her to sit. The heady perfume of the flowers that filled her arms was something Clare knew she would remember all the days of her life. She would never again inhale the fragrance of a rose without remembering the sweetness of this moment.

Adam went down on one knee and reached for her free hand, his warm brown eyes only inches from hers. "Let me start with an apology, Clare," he said softly. "Last night was a fiasco, and if I could erase it from your memory, I would. I knew I'd done a poor job, but Nicole pointed out in no uncertain terms just how badly I'd blown it. She read me the riot act, then kept after me until I finally told her what I should have told you. When I got done, she made me write it down so I would be sure to say it correctly tonight."

He reached into his pocket and withdrew a folded sheet of paper. "But you know something? I don't need this after all. Because these words were in my heart all along. I was just too afraid to say them. I was afraid I'd be rejected or made fun of, which is what my father did whenever I tried to tell him how I felt. That's a terrible legacy to give a child, and it has been a very, very difficult one to overcome.

"But I finally realized something last night. As long as I let what he did to me continue to affect my life, he still had control over me. And I decided I'm not going to give him that power anymore. Because I also realized that holding back doesn't protect your heart—it only alienates you from the people you love. It makes you isolated and lonely and empty."

He paused and drew a deep breath. "Clare, I told you last night that I'd like us to be a family. And that Nicole had come to care for you deeply. Those things are still true. But the main reason I want you to stay is far more selfish." He looked at her steadily, offering a clear view directly into his heart. "I love you, Clare. I love you more than life itself. And I can't imagine my future without you. Until you came, I existed in the shadows. I lived life, but only at the edges. I could never find a way to step into the sunlight. But you brought brightness and warmth to my world and gave me the courage to love."

He paused and reached into his pocket to withdraw a small square box, then flipped open the top to reveal a dazzling, heart-shaped diamond. "I chose this cut because I wanted it to symbolize my promise to you, Clare. For as long as I live, my heart will be yours. And I promise to always do my very best to share and to care and to love. Will you marry me?"

Clare stared at the sparkling diamond as the tears ran freely down her face. "Yes," she whispered. "Oh, yes!"

With unsteady fingers, Adam removed the ring from the box and took her left hand in his. Slowly he slid the band onto her finger. Then he stood and reached for her, drawing her to her feet. For a long moment they gazed at each other, and then his lips closed over hers in a kiss so tender, so full of promise, that she thought her heart would burst with happiness.

And in the moment before she lost herself in his embrace, Clare uttered a simple, silent expression of gratitude to the woman whose loving bequest had given two lonely people a second chance at love.

Thank you, Aunt Jo.

Epilogue

"Clare, have you talked with Seth Mitchell recently?"

She turned from watering the fern on the front porch to look at Adam, who had just retrieved the mail. "Yes. I called him a couple of days ago—the day after you gave me this." She held up her left hand with a smile and wiggled her fourth finger. "I told him that I'd completed the nanny assignment but that I was staying to take on a more permanent job."

Adam returned her smile, and the warmth in his unguarded eyes made her breath catch in her throat.

"That must be what this is about, then," he said, holding out a letter.

She put the watering can down and reached for the slim white envelope. When she slit the flap, a note fell out, as well as another envelope. Clare quickly scanned the note.

"Dear Mrs. Randall: Your aunt asked that I forward this to you after the six-month period stipulated in her will. My congratulations again to you and Dr. Wright. I wish you great happiness."

Clare set the note aside and turned her attention to the

smaller envelope, which was addressed to her and Adam in her aunt's flowing hand.

"Adam, this is for both of us. From Aunt Jo."

He stopped sorting the mail and walked over to her curiously. "Let's sit on the settee and read it together," he suggested.

Adam stole a quick kiss before he draped his arm around Clare's shoulders, and she gazed up at him longingly. "If we keep this up, we'll never get to Jo's letter," he teased.

Clare smiled. "Luckily we have a good chaperone."

Adam chuckled. "Too true. But I'm counting the days until you're living under our roof. In the meantime, my daughter is doing her job very diligently."

Clare nudged him playfully, then turned her attention back to the smaller envelope. Carefully she withdrew the single, folded sheet, then held it out so they could both scan it.

My dearest Clare and Adam,

If you are reading this, it means that Clare's nanny assignment has turned into something far more permanent. As I hoped it would.

Clare, you are a loving, sensitive, kind-hearted woman who has always had her priorities in order. The people you love have always come first in your life, and I greatly admired and respected the wonderful home you created for Dennis and David. I know their tragic deaths shattered your world in more ways than you ever spoke of. My heart ached for you, and I wanted desperately to help you find a way to recreate the kind of family you had lost.

That's where Adam came in. He has been a great friend to me for many years, and I have always considered him to be a fine man, with a tender heart and a great capacity to love. But because he carried his own scars, that capacity has never been realized. I knew it would take someone very special to reach him and to help him unlock his heart.

As I made the final revisions to my will, knowing that my earthly life was soon to end, I wanted to give you both a lasting gift. But what you needed most, Adam—help with Nicole so that the two of you could become a family—was not in my physical capacity to give. So I sent you Clare. I knew that her warm and loving heart could work miracles in your troubled relationship with Nicole. And I hoped, as time went by, that it would also work miracles in you so that, in the end, she would choose to give you a gift of her own—her love. In doing so, she would also fulfill my dearest wish for her—she would find a new home and a new family to love.

I cannot tell you how pleased I am that my wish came true. May your life together always be filled with joy, peace and hope. God bless you both. Aunt Jo.

As Clare finished reading the note, she reached up to brush the tears from her cheek. When she glanced at Adam, his eyes were suspiciously moist, as well.

"Did it ever occur to you that Aunt Jo had an ulterior motive for sending me here?" Clare asked softly.

Adam shook his head. "Never."

"But how could she have known this would happen?"

"Jo was a very astute lady. I guess she knew what we needed even better than we did. And you can't argue with success."

Clare smiled up at him tenderly. "I can think of lots better things to do than argue, anyway."

His eyes darkened, and he reached over to trace the elegant curve of her jaw. "Where's the chaperone?" he murmured.

"Cleaning up her room."

"Then we have plenty of time," he said.

"For what?"

"For this."

He drew her close, and as his lips claimed hers, Clare prayed that Aunt Jo knew the outcome of her carefully laid plans.

Because the ending wasn't just happy. It was, as she had hoped, a miracle.

Dear Reader,

As I write this letter, I am still enjoying the fragrance and beauty of eighteen long-stemmed roses that my husband sent me for my birthday. And I have to admit they helped inspire the last scene in this book! I am so very blessed to be married to a wonderful man who never hesitates to tell me how much he loves me, and who demonstrates that love in countless ways every day.

As Adam learns in this book, love can't exist in a vacuum. It must be nurtured constantly, and it requires sharing at the deepest, most intimate levels. That isn't always easy. But only when we let people into our hearts do we experience love in the fullest sense.

And that's true for any kind of love. Between man and wife, parents and children, brother and sister, and between friends. Love is a precious gift, one that far transcends the value of any material object. That's why Aunt Jo wanted to leave this enduring legacy to her three great-nieces. And as each comes to realize, love is the best gift of all.

Please join me in October for the final installment of the Sisters & Brides series, when Morgan meets her match on the rocky coast of Maine as she works to claim her legacy.

In the meantime, may all of you find the courage to open your hearts to love, and may your days be filled with joy and hope.

Irene Hannon

Look for A.J. and Clare's sister Morgan's story
THE UNEXPECTED GIFT
Available in October 2005
from Love Inspired Books.

Turn the page for a sneak peek...

Chapter One

"**Y**ou're working over Thanksgiving?"

Morgan Williams heard the surprise—and disapproval—in Grant Kincaid's voice, and frowned in annoyance. It was the same reaction she'd gotten from A.J., who had made it clear that she thought her sister was a workaholic without a life. Morgan hadn't liked it then. She didn't like it now.

"I happen to be committed to my job," Morgan replied stiffly. "In my world, working on holidays is a way of life. That's how you get ahead."

For a moment there was silence on the other end of the line, and Morgan fully expected the man to respond with some negative comment. But he surprised her by moving on.

"Well, just let me know when you plan to come up and I'll have Aunt Jo's cottage ready," he said.

"I'll do that. In the meantime, I'd like to get an appraisal done on the property."

Again, her comment was greeted with silence. When he did respond, there was a note of caution in his voice. "May I ask why?"

Morgan glanced at her watch impatiently. "Frankly, it will be extremely difficult for me to meet the residency stipulation in Aunt Jo's will. I have trouble taking off four days, let alone four weeks. So before I spend a lot of time and energy trying to figure out how to juggle my life to allow for several weeks in Maine, I want to make sure it's worth my while. Besides, we'll need to get an appraisal before we sell, anyway."

"You're planning to sell?"

At the censure—and shock—in his voice, Morgan's frown returned. "Of course. What would I do with a cottage in Maine?"

"Maybe the same thing your aunt did. Spend time here, relax, regain perspective. It's a beautiful spot."

Morgan gave a frustrated sigh. "I'm sure it's lovely, Mr. Kincaid. But as I explained, I have virtually no time for that kind of thing."

"The cottage was very special to your aunt."

"I understand that. But holding on to a place I'll never use doesn't make good business sense. You would certainly be welcome to buy my share at the end of six months, assuming I even make it that far."

"That's kind of you. But that property is way out of my price range."

Was there a touch of sarcasm in his comment? Morgan couldn't be sure but she didn't have time to waste wondering about it. She had a presentation to finalize for a meeting that would be starting in less than an hour. Further discussion of Aunt Jo's cottage would have to wait. "Look, I need to run. We can talk about that at some point in the future. In the meantime, can you take care of the appraisal?"

"Yes."

"Fine. I'll try to get up to Maine soon. The cottage looks to be about a four-hour drive from Boston. Is that right?"

"More like five, if you're not familiar with the back roads."

"Okay. I'll try to make a weekend trip soon."

"I'll look forward to it."

This time there was no mistaking the sarcasm in his tone. Nor the fact that he didn't think much of her priorities. Just like her sister. Come to think of it, he and A.J. would have been ideal co-owners of the cottage, Morgan thought wryly. Too bad Aunt Jo hadn't paired them up.

*And now turn the page
for a sneak preview of
DIE BEFORE NIGHTFALL
by Shirlee McCoy,
part of Steeple Hill's exciting new line,
Love Inspired Suspense!
On sale in September 2005
from Steeple Hill Books.*

Chapter One

She'd never hung wash out to dry, but that wouldn't keep her from trying. Raven Stevenson eyed the basket of sopping white sheets and the small buckets of clothespins sitting at her feet. How hard could it be?

Five minutes later she'd managed to trample one sheet into the mud. The other two were hanging, lopsided and drooping, from the line. "It could be worse, I suppose."

"Could be better, too." A pie in one hand, a grocery bag in the other, Nora Freedman came around the side of the house, her eyes laughing as she eyed the muddy sheet. "Never had to dry laundry the old-fashioned way, I see."

"I'm afraid not. I hope it won't take me long to get better at it."

"It won't. You wouldn't believe how many renters have turned away from this property just because I don't have a clothes dryer."

"Their loss. My gain."

Nora beamed at the words. "I knew it! Knew the minute I saw you, you were the person for this place. Here,

I've brought you a welcome gift. Pecan pie and some things to stock your cupboards."

"You didn't have to—"

"Of course I didn't. I *wanted* to. I'll leave everything in the kitchen. Gotta scoot. Prayer meeting in a half hour. Call me if you need something."

"I will. Thank you."

"See you at church Sunday? You did say you planned to attend Grace Christian?"

The nerves that Raven had held at bay for a week clawed at her stomach. "Yes. I'll see you then."

"I knew it. Just knew this would work out." Then she was gone as quickly as she'd come, her squat, squarish figure disappearing around the corner of the house.

In the wake of her departure the morning silence seemed almost deafening. Raven hummed a tune to block out the emptiness. Bending to lift the dirty sheet, her gaze caught and held by a strange print in the barren, muddy earth. A footprint—each toe clearly defined, the arch and heel obvious. Small, but not a child's foot. Someone had walked barefoot through the yard on a day when winter still chilled the air.

Who? Why? Raven searched for another print and found one at the edge of the lawn. From there, a narrow footpath meandered through sparse trees, the prints obvious on earth still wet from last night's rain. She followed the path until it widened and Smith Mountain Lake appeared, vast and blue, the water barely rippling. And there, on a rickety dock that jutted toward the center of the lake, her quarry. White hair, white skin, a bathing suit covering a thin back.

Raven hurried forward. "Are you all right?"

"Thea?" The woman turned, wispy hair settling in a

cloud around a face lined with age. "I've been waiting forever. Didn't we agree to meet at ten?"

Ten? It was past noon. Two hours was a long time to sit half-clad in a chilly breeze. Raven's concern grew, the nurse in her cataloguing what she saw—pale skin, goose bumps, a slight tremor. "Actually, I'm Raven. I live in the cottage up the hill."

"Not Thea's cottage? She didn't tell me she had guests."

"She probably forgot. Were you planning a swim?"

"Thea and I always swim at this time of year. Though usually it's not quite so cold."

"It *is* chilly today. Here put this on." Raven slid out of her jacket and placed it around the woman's shoulders.

"Do I know you?"

"No, we haven't met. I'm Raven Stevenson."

"I'm Abigail Montgomery. Abby to my friends."

"It's nice to meet you, Abby. Would you like to join me for tea? I've got a wonderful chamomile up at the house." Raven held out her hand and was relieved when Abby allowed herself to be pulled to her feet.

"Chamomile? It's been years since I've had that."

"Then let's go." Raven linked her arm through Abby's and led her toward the footpath, grimacing as she caught sight of her companion's scraped feet. Another walk through the brambles would only make things worse. "It looks like you've forgotten your shoes."

Abby glanced down at her feet, confusion drawing her brows together. Then she looked at Raven and something shifted behind her eyes as past gave way to present. Raven had seen it many times, knew the moment. Abby realized what had happened. She waited a heartbeat, watching as the frail, vague woman transformed into someone stronger and much more aware.

"I've done it again, haven't I?" The words were firm but Abby's eyes reflected her fear.

"Nothing so bad. Just a walk to the lake."

"Dressed in a bathing suit? In…" Her voice trailed off, confusion marring her face again.

"It's April. A lovely day, but a bit too cold for a swim."

"What was I thinking?" Frustration and despair laced the words.

"You were thinking about summer. Perhaps a summer long ago."

"Do I know you?"

"My name is Raven. I live up the hill at the Freedman cottage."

"Raven. A blackbird. Common. You're more the exotic type I'd think, with that wild hair and flowing dress."

Raven laughed in agreement. "I've been fighting my name my whole life. You're the first to notice."

"Am I? Then I guess I'm not as far gone as I'd thought." Despite the brave words, the tears behind Abby's eyes were obvious, the slight trembling of her jaw giving away her emotions.

Raven let her have the moment. Watched as she took a deep shuddering breath and glanced down at her bathing suit. "I suppose it could be worse. At least I wore clothes this time. Now, tell me, where are we headed?"

"To the cottage for tea."

"Let's go, then."

"Here, slip my shoes on first."

"Oh, I couldn't. What about you?"

"I've got tough skin." Raven slipped her feet out of open-heeled sneakers and knelt to help Abby slide her feet into them.

They made their way up the steep incline, Raven's hand steady against Abby's arm. It hurt to see the woman beside her. Hurt to know that a vital, lively woman was being consumed by a disease that would steal her essence and leave nothing behind but an empty shell. Why? It was a question she asked often in her job as a geriatric nurse. There was no answer. At least none that she could find, no matter how hard she prayed for understanding.

"Sometimes it just doesn't happen the way we want."

"What? Startled, Raven glanced at Abby.

"Life. It doesn't always work out the way we want it to. Sad, really. Don't you think?"

Yes. Yes, she did think it was sad. Her own life a sorry testament to the way things could go wrong. Raven wouldn't say as much. Not to Abby with her stiff spine and desperate eyes. Not to anyone. "It can be, yes. But usually good comes from our struggles."

"And just what good will come of me losing my marbles, I'd like to know?"

"We've met each other. That's one good thing."

"That's true. I've got to admit I'm getting tired of not having another woman around the house."

"Do you live alone?"

"Goodness, no. I forget things, you know. I live with... I can't seem to remember who's staying with me."

"It's all right. The name will come to you."

Abby gestured to the cottage that was coming into view. "There it is. I haven't been inside in ages. Have you lived here long?"

"I moved in this morning."

"You remind me of the woman who used to live here."

"Do I?"

"Thea. Such a lovely person. It's sad what happened. So sad...."

CELEBRATE LOVE WITH

Eight classic Love Inspired wedding stories repackaged in a special collector's-edition set for you to enjoy all over again.

Written by some of Love Inspired's best authors, the Ever After collection gives you the chance to own earlier works from your favorite writers!

Look for 4 Ever After titles in stores this August and 4 more this November!

On sale August

Black Hills Bride
His Brother's Wife
The Cowboy's Bride
To Love and Honor

On sale November

Wedding at Wildwood
The Troublesome Angel
A Family To Call Her Own
Ever Faithful

Steeple
Hill®

www.SteepleHill.com   EVERAFTER

Love Inspired

SUSPENSE
RIVETING INSPIRATIONAL ROMANCE

**August brings tales of romance and intrigue
featuring a smashing new miniseries
from RITA® Award finalist Colleen Coble
writing as Colleen Rhoads.**

WINDIGO
TWILIGHT

by COLLEEN *R*HOADS

GREAT LAKES LEGENDS: Stories of the past, crimes of the present

She's faced with her parents' suspicious deaths and an
inheritance left uncertain—someone or something
sinister is determined to stop Becca Baxter's
search for truth on her family's island.

Available at your favorite retail outlet.

Steeple
Hill®

www.SteepleHill.com   LISWTCR

Take 2 inspirational love stories FREE!

PLUS get a FREE surprise gift!

Mail to Steeple Hill Reader Service™

In U.S.
3010 Walden Ave.
P.O. Box 1867
Buffalo, NY 14240-1867

In Canada
P.O. Box 609
Fort Erie, Ontario
L2A 5X3

YES! Please send me 2 free Love Inspired® novels and my free surprise gift. After receiving them, if I don't wish to receive anymore, I can return the shipping statement marked cancel. If I don't cancel, I will receive 4 brand-new novels every month, before they're available in stores! Bill me at the low price of $4.24 each in the U.S. and $4.74 each in Canada, plus 25¢ shipping and handling and applicable sales tax, if any*. That's the complete price and a savings of over 10% off the cover prices—quite a bargain! I understand that accepting the books and gift places me under no obligation ever to buy any books. I can always return a shipment and cancel at any time. Even if I never buy another book from Steeple Hill, the 2 free books and the surprise gift are mine to keep forever.

113 IDN DZ9M
313 IDN DZ9N

Name	(PLEASE PRINT)	
Address	Apt. No.	
City	State/Prov.	Zip/Postal Code

Not valid to current Love Inspired® subscribers.

Want to try two free books from another series?
Call 1-800-873-8635 or visit www.morefreebooks.com.

* Terms and prices are subject to change without notice. Sales tax applicable in New York. Canadian residents will be charged applicable provincial taxes and GST. All orders subject to approval. Offer limited to one per household.

® are registered trademarks owned and used by the trademark owner and or its licensee.

INTLI04R   ©2004 Steeple Hill

SUSPENSE
RIVETING INSPIRATIONAL ROMANCE

August brings tales of romance and intrigue featuring a smashing new miniseries from Tracey V. Bateman.

Reasonable Doubt

by Tracey V. Bateman

The Mahoney Sisters: Fighting for justice and love

What happens when a man suspected of murder falls in love with the police officer who may have to bring him to justice?

Available at your favorite retail outlet.

Steeple Hill®

www.SteepleHill.com

LISRDTVB

Love Inspired®

ANOTHER BOOK IN THE

Tiny Blessings

SERIES!

BROUGHT TOGETHER BY BABY

BY

CAROLYNE AARSEN

Caring for her adopted sister while their mother received physical therapy seriously cut into workaholic Rachel Noble's fund-raising schedule. Yet taking the premature toddler for regular doctor visits was something Rachel could get used to, because the pediatrician was handsome Eli Cavanaugh. Being a temporary mommy made Rachel long for a family of her own…with Eli!

TINY BLESSINGS: Giving thanks for the neediest of God's children, and the families who take them in!

Don't miss BROUGHT TOGETHER BY BABY

On sale August 2005

Available at your favorite retail outlet.

www.SteepleHill.com

LIBTBB

Love Inspired

THE

Texas Hearts

SERIES BEGINS WITH...

A CERTAIN HOPE

BY

LENORA WORTH

April Maxwell was coming home to tend to her beloved father and his ranch. Falling for rancher Reed Garrison was not an option. Not again, anyway. Yet Reed was always there for April, helping out, supporting her—and hoping that this time April would want to stay and put down roots...with him!

Texas Hearts: Sometimes big love happens in small towns....

Don't miss A CERTAIN HOPE
On sale August 2005

Available at your favorite retail outlet.

www.SteepleHill.com

LIACH